Es'kia Mphahlele

Chirundu

Lawrence Hill & Co., Publishers, Inc.
Westport, Connecticut

First published by Ravan Press (Pty), Ltd.,
Johannesburg, South Africa

Library of Congress Cataloging in Publication Data

Mphahlele, Ezekiel.
   Chirundu.

   I. Title.
PR9369.3.M67C4   1981   823   80-81803
ISBN 0-88208-122-5 (pbk.)   AACR2

First U.S. Edition, November 1981
9 8 7 6 5 4 3 2 1

Lawrence Hill & Co., Publishers, Inc.
Westport, Connecticut 06880

Manufactured in the United States of America

for
Livie and Nzim

who were there
at the crossroads of exile
in the grey of a new dawn —
　　not yet for them
　　not yet for us
children of the long long southern
　　midnight

To the Reader

In August 1977, after twenty years of self-imposed exile from South Africa, Es'kia Mphahlele returned to his native land. Why he chose this path rather than continuing in exile, as did many of his compatriots, is eloquently expressed in the paragraphs which follow.

We lived nine years in west, east and central Africa, two years in France, and nine years in the United States. For five years out of the nine that we lived in the United States, my wife and I felt that we were irrelevant outside Africa. To whom was I teaching black literatures in the United States—people genuinely interested in Africa, or merely students wanting to pick up an exotic grade? Should I not be where black literatures are organized and taught as a functional and organic part of African development and located, therefore, where there is a living cultural forum for them—on its own native soil? Shouldn't I be spending the rest of my life contributing to this development of the African consciousness?

I had come into a line of tradition in America that had started long ago, and I could not grasp the American's cultural goals. I saw them as too fragmented for me to feel part of a unified purpose. I want to teach in a community whose cultural goals or aspirations I comprehend, because education is for me an agent of culture even as it is culture itself.

I could identify intellectually and emotionally with the black American's condition, but I could not in any tangible, particular way *feel* his history. And to be actively and meaningfully involved in a people's concerns and political struggle as a genuine participant, you should *feel* its history. On the contrary, I kept feeling that *that* river was passing me by. Its complexity defies the oversimplification contained in "I am Black". And one thing I dislike is intellectual dishonesty, faked involvement that has only repeated slogans to subsist on. I had to return home if I wanted to teach in a situation whose cultural goals I understood. I am a teacher through and through, and I can't help it.

A secondary but still important reason was tied up with my "reluctance" to be sucked into the American thing. As long as I was in this frame of mind, I was not going to create fiction out of the American experience. I have abandoned myself to the tyranny of place, and as long as I do not have that sense of place, as long as I cannot remember a place by its smells and the texture of its life, I cannot create a sustained literary work out of it. South Africa, and Africa generally, still claimed me. Fiction depends a lot on particularities of place, and I would have to be back home to write fiction.

Anywhere in Africa? No. I had learned enough about Kenya and Zambia to realize that foreign Africans are welcome in only a very few African countries. Nigeria would have been a possibility, because I did spend four of the happiest and most fulfilling years of my exile there. Nigeria, Ghana and other West African countries restored to me the Africa that the sheer struggle for survival in South African ghetto life had stowed away in the deeper vault of my subconscious. But I was in West Africa before the revolutions, and today wouldn't know the present state of things.

An affectionate friend of mine invited me to come to Ghana in 1976, to settle. His country was then preparing for civilian government. I felt pretty bad about having to decline. But I could, I can, no longer afford to be adventurous.

In the years I was in Kenya (1963-66) several South African refugees who landed at Nairobi airport were sent off on the next plane to return to their initial host countries. Or else they were told to pass on to any other country of their choice. Several times the late Mr. Tom Mboya, then a cabinet minister, intervened, but the refugees would still be given a limited time to stay in Nairobi while they sought another way out.

At no time while I directed Chemchemi Creative Center in Nairobi did government officials come to our performances and art exhibitions when we invited them. And yet they went to performances and art exhibitions held at the National Theatre, Stanley Hotel, Donovan Mawle Theatre, which were then colonial institutions run by English expatriates. Chemchemi promoted indigenous arts whereas the others staged shows imported from the West End in London with white artists. Of course, these highly placed patrons would still have displayed a neo-colonial attitude if a Kenyan were running the creative center. But a South African establishing and directing the center accentuated the snobbishness.

In the Zambia of 1968-71 a number of refugees from South Africa, Angola, Mozambique, Rhodesia-that-was were held in prison for several months because they did not possess the "proper papers". The rationale was that if they were not attached to any of the political movements, they *had* to be "spies". Several teachers and a Namibian medical doctor had their residence permits terminated. They automatically lost their work permits and were packed off. In protest against this treatment of refugees, I broke my five-year contract at the University of Zambia after serving two years. My discussions with high government officials, at their own invitation, failed to produce any positive results in this whole business.

In several other countries where there were refugees and exiles, e.g., Tanzania, Malawi, Uganda, the heads of state and cabinet ministers might welcome us, but invariably the bureaucrats dispensed their own kind of "justice," unchecked. They blocked every possible approach that could gain you audience with the head of state. You had to quit in utter despair. This worked havoc particularly among refugees who had a profession to pursue.

In the Ghana of Nkrumah's days there was one white South African marxist who successfully instigated the government to get tough with refugees and exiles because we were "bourgeois". We offered our services there, asking to be regarded as Africans who should *not* be paid the expatriate allowances and gratuities enjoyed by white expatriates. In each African country where we lived South African exiles asked not to be treated as expatriates. This request was invariably rejected, and we were placed on expatriate contracts. When our services were terminated, white expatriates were taken in our place. It became quite clear that as an exile from another part of Africa you were too much on the host country's conscience: you could not easily be retrenched to make way for a national citizen qualified for the job. But there was not likely to be any such problem in terminating a white person's services at the end of a contract.

It has to be admitted that exiles are not per se the exemplary pick of any bunch anywhere in the world. South African exiles have been known to demand excessive attention from their host countries; the ones who have come out since 1976 have been known to despise the masses among whom they moved; they have been known to dictate the terms of where they shall be located in the host country. Other refugees from other parts of Africa have been thrown up by events, by a crisis, and overnight they are foreigners: they naturally are unprepared for the psychological trauma of being in an environment where they are unknown, where no one is going to fuss over them.

All the same, the lesson came painfully home to us that although an exile may accept the fact that he should not try to live on his own terms, this realization did not help him to deal with the more bitter facts: (a) that he cannot defend himself against mistreatment in the host country with the weapons of his choice, and (b) that there is for him no court of appeal.

Why, then, would I return to a country whose political administration I abhor? Why return to a system of education for Africans that I attacked and from which I was banned before I left in September 1957? Because it is still home, because there is a community to bolster my morale and my wife's, such as there isn't elsewhere. Our exit in 1957 was not a flight in the sense of a refugee's escape. I had a valid South African passport. Somewhere in the back of our minds we knew we would want to return. If I had not been banned, I would have continued to teach in a system I hated—because I had confidence that I could give more to the kids than the inferior syllabuses and curricula allowed. I would endure until something burst. What I mean is that our teachers should hang in there, because without the *good* teachers, the kids are left in the wilderness. As it is, they are learning enough to know that they are being cheated, and we now see them as a living evidence of the fact that the mind is a dangerous thing to experiment with. A good education sets up a divine discontent; a poor education, especially of a racist kind, sets up discontents that breed defiance.

I am an African humanist and an empiricist, as well as an idealist. I can function here in South Africa, and am no worse off than the rest of the oppressed millions. Compromises? Life for an oppressed person is one long, protracted, agonizing compromise. I didn't make any promises not to do this or that in order to be let in again. It hasn't been easy finding a job. I went through all the stages of influx-control procedures — screening for employment and residence in an urban area, which by definition is a "white area." You live in a ghetto, and that's a compromise you have to live with while still functioning. You have no freedom of mobility, and there are several compromises arising from that. I was refused a position as chairman of English at the University of the North, and I am teaching in a predominantly white university—but so were Denver and Pennsylvania universities! But I can do a lot of community work—teaching and conducting writers' workshops—and the University of the Witwatersrand lets me engage in several other educational projects unrelated to its own programs. That's a compromise I can live with and exploit, one I can deal with because I am now a member of a community. I believe that no matter what white people do to us, our ultimate goal is bigger than they are, than even *we* are, and therein lies the moral of my homecoming.

I got to know, when I was in the United States that an academic can, if he likes, lose himself in intellectual pursuits, move only in the university community, and be insulated from the rest of the larger community out there, safe, cozy, contented. I didn't want that to happen to me. I didn't want my self-respect to hang on the thin thread of long-distance commitment.

I also realize the longer I was away from here, the angrier, the more outraged, I felt against the sufferings of people here. Out of sheer impotence. In a sense, my homecoming was another way of dealing with impotent anger. It was also a way of extricating myself from twenty years of compromise, for exile is itself a compromise. Indeed, exile had become for me a ghetto of the mind. My return to Africa was a way of dealing with the concrete reality of blackness in South Africa rather than with the phantoms and echoes that attend exile.

ES'KIA MPHAHLELE

Chirundu

Children's Playsong

Sung while rope-skipping. A long rope is held at either end by a boy or girl. Groups of four to five boys and girls skip as the rope beats the earth.

In Tumbuka we say *sato,*
Nsato in Chinyanja.
Mama I'm afraid of the python,
I fear *nsato*, Mama.

Stay away from the python, child,
Stay away from *nsato*, child.
I'm afraid of *nsato*, Mama.

When you find it on its ground
You'll know the size of your fear —
So long, so heavy and wild.
Mama, I fear the python.

If he comes at you, my child,
To wrap you up in his coils,
And flicks a tongue of fire
And means you ill, my child,
Go burn his house down,
Burn down his house, my child,
And let him wander, far and wild.

No more will I fear him, Mama,
No more, no more.

Come away, my child,
Come away.
He's the king of all.

'Next time you scream like that in bed I'll turn the hose on you, you hear me! I hear in your countries the white man splices your balls in the jails. It's like a picnic for you here. One country, one nation, Kwacha! You there from South Africa, just you scream again and disturb other people in their sleep, you'll shit bricks. And you there the man from Zimbabwe, muttering to yourself won't help you one bit. One country! I know when you two meet out here in the yard you're badmouthing me and this country. We've given you sanctuary and saved you from life in the streets begging for food and shelter. Back in your own countries you'd be shitting bricks. One nation! Kwacha! Kwacha!'

The prison warder knocks his heels together and marches away in military fashion.

'What's come over him this time?' Chieza, the man from Zimbabwe, says.

Pitso, the man from South Africa, snorts. 'Twenty-seven months in this hole and the pink-assed baboon calls it sanctuary! Arrest refugees for entering the country without passports and visas, pretend they are spies for white governments, detain them without trial and then tell them you're giving them protection! Two years we've been in this hole!'

'Keep your gall bladder in check, your ulcer will be acting up again,' Chieza cautions. 'Anyhow that baboon has said it so often, and we've complained so often, it's like we're singing blues. Your bowels — have they worked this morning?'

'No, maybe that's why that man crawls up my spine so.'

'He's always doing it; you mustn't let it get in the way of your bow-

1

els. Before you attend to any illness —'

'My uncle always said,' Pitso recited the rest, 'clean up your bowels. That's where most troubles begin.'

There is not a single day when Chieza does not ask Pitso if his bowels have moved. The warder does not always start his ranting first thing in the morning. He simply shouts, 'Kwacha!' — *wake up, it's a bright new day!* Pitso will say almost as many times to Chieza, 'Five years after independence the baboon's ass is still bawling *kwacha!* Why?'

And Chieza will reply in his typical deep-thinking manner, 'Maybe it's always a bright new day for him and he's still in love with his clothes in this independence jive.'

The dozen prisoners under detention move into the yard to loll about while the native inmates go about their assigned jobs. Previously the warder came to taunt them during the noon meal. Of late he is in the habit of haranguing the detainees first thing in the morning like an addict who has to slug down a drink to start the day. This, because Pitso's nightmares are becoming more frequent. He jumps from his bunk as if it were the middle one or the highest, beats on the steel door and cries like a wounded bull. And Chieza will always begin the day's conversation with 'How are the bowels — have they worked?'

In the twenty-seven months they have been in detention, Pitso has put on plenty of fat. To see him now you wouldn't think he used to be slender. His nervous condition has deteriorated since he skipped the western border of his country. Chieza believes firmly that frequent bowel movements can set Pitso right. This hasn't happened so far, although their friends Moyo and Studs never allow his supply of purgative to run out.

The country allows refugees to stay in the country as long as they are kept in camps and cared for by their organizations. Chieza and Pitso and their fellow detainees arrived unattached. They must be spies, the immigration authorities concluded. There is no proof either way, so they must be detained indefinitely. The other detainees have come from Namibia, Angola and Mozambique.

'What's there in this country to spy about?' Pitso often rails. 'Why would a white government trust a black man to bring back information when there are so many whites here they can send? Information about what? *Hela,* security is as tight in this country as the asshole of a skunk! These South African whites working in the copper mines, these British and American expatriates — they could bomb any building here in broad daylight if they had a mind to it.'

'No use, no use,' Chieza coaxes.

'Know what I dreamt about last night? This country was on fire. A real fire I mean. Blazing all over. Only reason it didn't spread into Zimbabwe, it was stopped by the Zambesi. The hippos were screaming and moaning like the water itself was on fire. I came within an inch of the jaws of a hippo when I started out of bed screaming.'

Chieza shakes his head slowly, his face a picture of a thousand misfortunes. 'Some day it will happen,' he says gravely, and goes on to pull out the hairs from his cheeks.

'Moffat Chieza! Moffat Chieza! Pitso Mokae! Pitso Mokae!'

'There goes the baboon!' Pitso says with a deep sigh. 'I used to think those whites back home were the lost link, but *this!* I don't think there are any cliffs left in this world that could hold him.'

'No use, no use,' Chieza says as he stands up, making his way to the baboonery, as the detainees call the warder's office. 'I know it must only be the paper, although the donkey would like to see us both come to carry it.'

'Good luck, greetings to you both! Moyo and Studs.' Chieza reads out the words handwritten on the front page of *Capricorn*. 'Wonder why they didn't come yesterday,' he mumbles.

Yesterday was Sunday. About twice a month Moyo and his friend Studs come to visit the two. Studs's younger brother and Pitso were schoolmates in Johannesburg. Studs preceded them at Fort Hare College by a few years. He lost no time in going to the Central Prison after he had read of the arrest and detention of Chieza and Pitso by order of the then Minister of Internal Affairs, Chimba Chirundu. For two years Studs and his friend Moyo have made it a habit to visit on Sundays when they can, but they take turns to bring the detainees the Sunday issue of *Capricorn*. There have been intermittent periods of intensive activity outside on behalf of the detainees. As when a representative of the United Nations Commission for Refugees, or Amnesty in Britain, or a native lawyer shuffles papers and strides noisily in and out of the hallways of power and pleads and pleads and argues. Opinion heaves and sighs and moans and switches off, to be recharged and set on the same cycle again. All to no avail.

'Hei, hei! That fellow's case is on in a fortnight,' Chieza shouts.

'Who?'

'Chirundu, who else?'

'I used to hate that chimp after he put us in the jug,' Pitso says. 'Now the mention of his name bores me. Like I had nothing any more

3

inside me to hate him with. Then he's arrested for bigamy, and d'you think I've anything left to gloat with? Niks. Just contempt. You know I've come to believe contempt is more satisfying, maybe even more dignified than hate?'

'Bigamy, bigamy,' Chieza says, as if he has been listening to his own private conversation. 'What a petty thing for a Cabinet Minister to be hauled up for.'

'That's part of the reason for my contempt, see. Why would the blinking idiot go and legalize a city piece when he could have access to it without all that paper and dotted line and ring stuff? The people who'll be looking on must think him an ass because they have extra-mural interests all over the place while they play the dutiful husband and father. Why would the daffer do this kind of thing, why?'

'The way I read you the line between contempt and sympathy is very, very thin.'

Pitso continues to stare into the daylight.

'Tirenje, Tirenje,' Chieza repeats the name, savouring the sound. 'What a beautiful sound, that. TI-REN-JE!'

'Eh? Chirundu's first wife — or the second?'

'The first, and is she moving against him! You remember *she* brought up the case against the chimp through the General Attorney. She must be beautiful, with a name like that — Tirenje, Tirenje. Kind of name you feel you can sleep with. I'd like to meet her.'

'Who's the second woman by the way?'

'Let's see. Monde. Four years younger than Tirenje. Wait a minute — yes. The honourable the minister is 37, Tirenje 32, Monde 28.'

'Just your age, you and me,' Pitso observes, thinking aloud. And he goes and does some such fool thing.' After a moment's pause he says, 'Tell me, Chieza, son of Africa, why do I get all riled up about this? He's no relative or friend of mine.'

'He's your enemy, chum, and yet one would think you were concerned for him, the way you carry on.'

'Just my madness.'

'I'll say!'

CHIRUNDU

April 1, morning

Chimba Chirundu, accused, sits near his advocate, Mr Clare, his face a picture of disgust and boredom. Every so often the flesh under his jaws pushes out and downward, like a fat child who is sulking and is set on a course of non-collaboration. His jaws are prominent under the ears, and you can see distended veins bunched around those protuberances which tell you he is biting and rubbing his molars together. Like a man who is feeling cold. Which cannot be: these are typically mellow days of a Central African autumn.

Chirundu's face is a smooth velvety black. His eyes sit deep in his skull and his beetling brows give him the expression of a creature stalking another, biding its time. And yet he is actually bored and resentful. You could pull him through the eye of a needle, so slick and cool is he dressed. This morning it took him no less than twenty minutes deciding which suit to put on — sports wear to show his spite, or a London suit to prove he was not to be ruffled by the proceedings? He settled on a suit. He orders his suits from Durham's in London. Most of his garments in fact. Out to beat the mercantile system. West Germany sends its poorest men's underwear which tears after the first wash. The Indian tailors give you the poorest cloth imaginable at prices that insult your intelligence — ridiculously high. Spinach, as the local people call the material. He will yet be the instrument of their expulsion, the curry-eating species, Chirundu swears privately. That South African Jew, too, who sells American clothes at prices that scream like an express train that is never going to stop at your station. No better than the rest of them, the Jew. We'll nail him one of these days. Chummy with the Vice

President, too — invites big government people to his estate for Sunday picnic lunches and champagne. Around a pool no one swims in. A life style he has brought with him from South Africa . . .

Chimba stands tall. There is something of the aristocrat about him. He drives a large Mercedes. He is Minister of Transport and Public Works. The editor of *Capricorn,* the government-owned paper, suggested that the Minister be suspended until the end of the trial should determine his guilt or innocence. The editor was sacked; Chimba kept his post while on bail. 'I was destined for great things,' he keeps saying to himself.

In the people's court convened this first day of April, 1969, Chimba Chirundu, hereinafter called the accused, is charged with the crime of bigamy in that on or about the 23rd May, 1968, the accused did wrongfully and unlawfully go through a form of marriage under Ordinance 058 of 1926 as amended in Act 5 of 1965 with one Monde Lundia in contravention of 3(i)(c) read with Sections 4(a), 5(c), 7 and 8 of the same Act, the accused being at all material times legally married to one Tirenje Mirimba in accordance with the requirements of Section 1 of the aforementioned Act, which marriage still subsists. Wherefore, upon the proof and conviction thereof, Attorney General for the Southern Province prays the judgment of the Court against the accused, according to law.

Not guilty.
May it please your lordship, I appear for the accused in this case.
Swear in the witness.
. . . the truth, the whole truth, and nothing but the truth.
Your name is Kasoka . . .
Yes.
You are Bemba by tribe?
I am.
You know a lot about Bemba customary law?
Yes.
How can you substantiate that?
I know it from the time I was still hanging in my father's b . . . — I mean when I was still in my mother's womb. (Giggles in the court.)
Tell the court what Bemba law says concerning marriage.
Witness Kasoka explains. The girl's parents will accept a gift from the suitor if they want him for a son-in-law. They will decline it if they

are not in favour. Then the bride price. How can the marriage be registered? In a local court. A receipt is given. Registration at a local court is to give proof you are eligible for a municipal house as a married couple. Registration under the Ordinance kills and supersedes customary marriage.

Europeans divorce. Do the Bemba?

It is not easy to get divorce in Bemba law. First thing is separation when the man packs off the wife to her parents or when the parents collect her at her request. She cannot of her own accord go to her parents. They would send her back to her husband, or tell her to go to the local court to complain. The parties may patch things up again or divorce will follow if parents on both sides have failed to reconcile them.

Chirundu's mind beats back and forth between present and past. Kasoka bores him. He resents this whole business. But he must wait his turn as the accused. The idiots, I'll tell them where to get off! They can't haul a Cabinet Minister before a public court like a commoner. I'll make *that* clear to the fatheads! I was destined for great things . . .

Is there support for the wife after divorce?

Yes.

Repeat to the court what you said earlier. Do you mean that even when one has gone through customary form, once one registers a marriage under the Ordinance as we know it in the Statute Book, this latter will supersede customary marriage whether or not such a union has been recorded in a local office for house allocation?

Yes, Sir.

Is this generally known among the Bemba people?

Yes, it is, especially the educated ones, and the Christians.

In the towns, do people still conform to this pattern?

Yes, Sir. There is also a form of marriage we call *chakutula*, contracted in a town away from the girl's parents. A provisional thing only. To make it valid the parents have to accept *ntsalamu*, the gift.

When do the Bemba consider a divorce is inevitable in traditional life?

When the people on either side refuse to talk and therefore attempts at reconciliation fail. Then the gift must be returned.

Defence Advocate may cross-examine, my lord.

Any questions, Mr Clare?

If your lordship pleases. Perhaps you can help the court, Mr Kasoka, by telling us what happens in Bemba customary law if either a man or his wife leaves the common home and decides to get married, without having gone through the procedures you have mentioned in answer to the State Advocate's questions. The party that remarries is no longer interested in the original marriage — am I right? Does the marriage come to an end?

It stops.

What do you mean? — That it amounts to a divorce?

It must. But the first marriage remains. I mean the marriage under the white man's Ordinance, if this has been followed in the first place.

But surely there is no bigamy in Bemba custom, is there?

No.

You have said that registration in the Boma or local court is not the same as that under the Ordinance?

Yes, I have.

So that if the accused says that as far as he knows the marriage between him and Tirenje Mirimba was under Bemba law, and stopped when Tirenje Mirimba left their home, you would not quarrel with that?

Well there is the Ordinance —

I'm not talking about the Ordinance. I'm talking about Bemba traditional law. You're no authority on marriage under the Ordinance, are you?

No.

Now you, if your wife, married by Bemba law, deserted you, would you, would you not feel free to marry another woman, either by traditional or any other law? Tell me, would you not feel free to do that? Would you as Bemba feel you were committing bigamy?

No.

The accused is going to say that when he married Monde Lundia, he did not know his marriage to Tirenje Mirimba was still in force. Would you consider that belief unreasonable?

I don't know.

Come, Mr Kasoka. You are contradicting yourself. Have you not just said you would not feel bound to a marriage that did not work because the wife left the house?

Yes.

I have no further questions, my lord.

Attorneys-at-law, monkeys-at-law on April fool's day! My advocate knows I knew the first marriage was still in force. But he says something entirely the opposite. That's the line of arguement he chooses to present. Well, that's what lawers are for — to get you out of a mess no matter what it costs, whoever pays.

'You can't go into that court, Mr Chirundu, and plead guilty.' That's what he said to me. 'You'll be convicted and stripped of your post in the government and maybe on the Central Committee of the National Alliance Party.'

'You think I don't know that? Look, Mr Clare, your people colonized this country and imposed their own laws on us. Now the Ordinance supplants native customary law. And yet the British kept the tribal system alive so as to be able to govern through chiefs and kings. Isn't that contradictory? I'm out to fight a system. The Ordinance should recognize traditional marriage as something that cannot be superseded, because we are polygamous. I don't know if you understand me, Mr Clare. I don't want to plead guilty, I want to speak up so that when the government gets around to marriage laws this inanity will not be repeated.'

'But you married the first Mrs Chirundu under the Ordinance.'

'You forgot I registered the marriage first in the local court before we went to the Ordinance.'

'What was the point, if you knew the Ordinance would declare the customary union null and void?

'Because I wanted to test the validity of the Ordinance in the matter and my instincts told me I was doing the right thing.'

'Mr Chirundu, that method of testing a law is for the hoi polloi. A civil servant like you — a VIP at that — cannot test a law by breaking it. You comply and then fight it with the legal weapons you have, through parliamentary processes.'

'British mentality!'

'It's a British-based Ordinance we're faced with. This is British law and a British kind of legislature we're dealing with in this country.'

I couldn't argue any further. How could I make Clare *feel* what went on inside me in those days of beautiful dreams and initiation into the ecstasies of feminine companionship? Questions are asked and pass unanswered, then one forgets the questions. Answers are given and they too are forgotten. Nothing else at the moment seems important. Not even the vows, private or public.

I did not see Tirenje outside the courthouse this morning. I lingered outside, eager but not eager to see her. I still love her. In a different way. I don't brood much. I take circumstances in stride and keep moving on, dealing with the present. Maybe because I can't deal with the past. To a politician like me, the present is all important. The past can be a luxury for dopes like the Vice President, who keeps harping on culture, culture, culture, or *cuchah,* as he says it. No, I don't express myself right. I think the past is important only in as far as it becomes a servant of the present.

Why, then, did I marry by traditional law if this is what I think about the past? I regard marriage as a very personal thing. If our traditional systems do not stand in the way of our progress as a people, and if the individual is best fulfilled when he orders his life according to traditional custom, let the past stay with us. A man's connection with his ancestors is a personal one. Let him stay with them if he wants to. I registered our marriage under the Ordinance after being married in the local court by customary law to satisfy Tirenje, who was emphatic in saying, 'I don't hold with polygamy.' In a sense, this court farce was predictable. And yet it was not. I could never have thought Tirenje capable of bringing a criminal charge against me. And yet she had given me a signal that should have told me she was not going to tolerate the situation long. I thought the most she would do would be to sue for divorce. It would have been a privately settled case. I would simply support her and the children, out of charity. Later I realized that the divorce proceedings would reveal the thing that has brought all this about.

'Drop this silly charge, Wanika,' I said to the Prosecutor, Che Chimimba — Mr Big Stomach, as he's called in court circles. I said, 'Drop the case, man, what have you to gain? This is not the kind of case that could win you laurels — domestic squabble, that's all it is.' This was after I had received the summons.

He looked me straight in the face out of those big bulging eyes. 'Nothing,' he answered. 'I just enjoy seeing rats like you scurrying about when the law seeks you out. You're aware we never liked each other, Chirundu, mighty Chirundu, who can't settle his domestic squabbles without breaking the law.'

'I never pretended it was otherwise.'

'So, you think because you're a minister you can go about playing with women's hearts. Hit and run, we call it. So climb down and run out captain, the people are attacking the caravan!'

'The transport workers are threatening a strike. Isn't that enough to keep me worried without this stupid trial? Did you set the trial at this time in order to have me discredited?'

'Mr Chirundu, you don't seem to realize that a civil servant has a private and a public life. What you do about a strike has nothing to do with your marital problems.'

10

'These are marital problems imposed upon us by the Europeans and you've become their puppet to make sure we're never going to be totally free.'

'Oh these dialectics bore me. You are a politician and I'm a Prosecutor who must ensure the law is not flouted for the purpose either of taking advantage of the weak and defenceless or subverting the honest work of those in authority. As a politician you can abolish any law perhaps, but I'd like to see you dare tinker with this one.'

That man, o that man . . . how we hate each other . . . !

Next to this huge wagon of a man, everybody else in the court looked small and unimportant. I knew Che Chimimba would be the last person to drop a case like this. I just wanted to be sure I had a full-blooded enemy to contend with. I'm sure he enjoyed the game. A criminal case against a Cabinet Minister! Milk and honey were being offered him to eat and swim in. That blustering hippo!

So the case was just a performance. If I didn't know Wanika the Prosecutor hated me so much, for reasons that would be tedious to recount, I would have wondered why he was straining so hard to make it look like the trial of the half-century. He certainly wanted a show. I was in an awkward position: all the press publicity and talk among bar-crawling drunks was damaging to my political life. 'You stay on,' the President said, 'and we'll see how the trial ends. If you lose, you know you cannot stay in the Cabinet. Your position in the Central Committee will depend on what the majority of our comrades think.'

Deadpan language, giving no indication of what he felt about *me*. I can never understand it, somehow. The President trembles with emotion when he talks to the nation about something that moves him deeply. Then he swallows saliva at short intervals as if he were suppressing tears. And now he talks to me like an English school principal.

Anyhow, let the press and the pub-crawlers amuse themselves as much as they want. This they must bear in mind: they are dealing with Chimba Chirundu. If I didn't know the outcome of the trial beforehand, I'd be kicking my heels and talking endlessly to people to find some reassurance. If the judge issues an option of a fine, it will suit me good! I've already found out that the maximum sentence is twelve months. That would slow me down. But I can survive it. I'll come back fighting. I know I've the edge on a number of the fellows in the Cabinet. I have drive, I'm like a cross-country runner. I may start late — indeed I *was* a late starter — but I stay on the course, and I know I'll get to the finish.

I don't have to worry about a government house being taken over. Because I live in my own house. Build your own house, Chimba, a little voice whispered to me. You never know when there'll be a coup and then where will you be? So I had a house built as soon as I was taken into the Cabinet. Monde will not need to fear eviction.

I wonder how the two — Tirenje and Monde — will behave when they see each other? They met once. Quarrelled and nearly came to blows.

For some odd reason Monde often said how she would like to meet Tirenje. 'Why?' I'd ask. 'Just to see her, of course. Don't you know a woman has a burning curiosity to see the person whose place she has taken in a husband's heart? Tell me, why don't you divorce her?' 'Because *I'm* the deserter, technically. Besides, I *want* to keep two wives — one who meets my demands in political life *and* in the city, the other in the country for whenever I tour the rural areas.' 'But you're more here than there.' 'Just keep your mind on your own interests, young woman!'

Yes, I'll come back fighting. They'll know it! Politics is my life. I don't have more than a teacher's certificate. The only thing I could do professionally if I were kicked out of politics would be to teach. Who wants to sink so low in income after a good government job? Also, politics is a game you teach yourself. It's your effort, your instincts, your mind, your energy, your vanity that go into the training. You don't prepare for it, you learn by doing it. You've got to be wholly in it or out. It's not a missionary venture, not a Baden-Powell affair. You've got to be bold enough to lie, and when you are found out be bold enough to say 'Ladies and gentlemen, the circumstances are now different.' How could you quit something you'd invested so much of *yourself* in? Yes, you invest a lot of yourself in teaching, too, but you work under a headmaster who is also a servant of the government. My only boss is the President. Between me and him is a vast area in which I can express myself. I love to influence people — adults I mean. I love power. I think I'm learning how to handle it. Have it I must! And I was destined for great things . . .

I have seen weak people at too close a range to feel anything but contempt for them. My grandfather, my father often told me, was a strong-willed man. If he found someone else's cattle in his maize field he warned the owner. If he found them the second time he hacked their legs with a chopper and told the owner to come and collect them. He would always make sure he had a witness when he issued a warning. So the king's council would have no choice but to acquit him. Grandfather was also an astute warrior. I'm told after I had been born, he held me in his arms and said, 'This boy shall bear my name, Chimba. He shall walk straight as a bluegum tree and yield no ground to anyone but his king. I can see him standing on that hill there against the growing light of a new dawn. And he will tell the people to wake up for a new day has come . . .'

Yes, when my people moved against British rule, I was one of those who led the National Alliance Party to carry the message of hope throughout the country, shouting *Kwacha!* — a bright new day. How real grandfather's words were to become. He died before my eyes were open.

Between my father, now eighty-one, and me, the field has widened. He is strong-willed, yes, but just for the sake of being so. The kind of man villagers speak of as being stubborn, with the implication that they cannot work with him, they can do nothing with him. Over the last ten years, since I got married to Tirenje, we have always talked at cross-purposes with father. As a result, my visits to his house at Shimoni on the edge of the Copperbelt have become fewer and fewer. Of late, he has taken Tirenje's side in our separation.

Back in 1954 I began to teach in a secondary school of the Seventh Day Adventist Church in Kapiri. Kapiri is on the line of rail from the south to the north, and is two hundred miles from Shimoni, which lies north east. I taught history and Bemba and Nyanja. This was a big school of some eight hundred children. About three-quarters were the primary-school section, a quarter made up the secondary division.

I had taught during the year 1951 in the primary department. Just after the Great Drought, which made it impossible for me to finish high school. In 1952-1953 the school had sponsored my teacher training at their 'normal' institution near the Nyasaland border. It was here that I perfected my Nyanja. One of these days I was going to move into Lozi and maybe even Tonga, I kept promising myself. That was me: I loved languages. Think what I could do, how far I could spread myself riding on four languages. My passion for history was also confirmed. I was then qualified to teach secondary school. Kapiri took me back in 1954. But not before I signed an agreement that I would serve them for a minimum of five years.

As you taught different classes, you were assigned a class to look after. You called the register here and you compiled the pupils' records. It was this class, which I also taught history, that a girl of remarkable ability joined in the following year. She was seventeen. A girl with a striking face. Pretty, too, without looking precious and dainty, such as one commonly sees among townbred girls. She also joined my Nyanja class. A teacher will always find a pupil who is more easily accessible than the average, whom he can more readily trust with small errands and chores, whom he can more readily ask. Tirenje was such a pupil.

Mission boarding schools always had staff houses on their property to make conditions look more attractive to prospective applicants who lived outside Kapiri. It was custom to assign for manual work sessions once a week the cleaning of quarters for bachelor staff. Spinsters on the staff often cleaned their own quarters or made other independent arrangements. I used to give Tirenje the task of cleaning my two-roomed 'house'. She liked to do it. A little shy, but not timid. A girl of country breeding with an earthy voice. Although her face was youthful her eyes seemed to hold unutterable wisdom. No, she was not timid, like a deer that will bolt as soon as you touch it.

Often she asked me if she might go to the market for me, whenever the matron of her hostel sent her to buy her things. And yet she didn't strain at being obliging.

If I found Tirenje cleaning the room, which became more and more frequent, I sat on my bed. I would watch her every movement — so sturdy, so very much together. That compact peasant form under the school uniform — a white blouse and black 'gym dress' — those sturdy bare clean legs; the firm hips; those clam eyes that neither deny you nor sell anything; those firm undelivered breasts — all of her, set me on fire. I felt as if my brain had abdicated its role of monitor, disclaiming all responsibility for anything that might happen.

'Let me explain the errors in your history test, Tirenje,' I said when she was about to leave.

'Yes, Sir,' she said as she curtseyed.

'Come and sit on my bed.'

She stopped halfway between the bed and the centre of the room, leaning slightly against the table I used both as working and dining furniture.

'Come, do not be afraid, I do not eat people.'

She took one step, and then another, her two hands touching as if to assume a posture of supplication. A posture that was never arrived at because the two hands were raised to the side for her fingertips to scratch the lobe of an ear.

'Come on.'

'Yes, Sir.' She sat next to me. I opened the exercise book and began to explain.

She needed to read more carefully the section of her textbook dealing with the American revolution. 'George Washington, the Boston Tea Party. Why would the American people not let the tea into the country? Why did the British consider it was of the utmost importance to hold on to American territory? Things like that, you see what I mean? Right. It is all there in the book . . .'

'Yes, Sir.'

'You understand, don't you?'

'Yes, Sir, I do.'

'And you know that once you have written your final examination and finished here it will not matter one bit whether or not the Americans poured out the tea into the Atlantic, whether or not some adventurer called George Washington ever lived — you know that, don't you? The British have waged too many wars for us to bother about this single one. What is it to us? But we must know these things. The syllabus says we must, Amen. You must pass your examination, and I am going to help you all the way. Survive. Here we are learning about the American Revolution and our children do not know where our people came from, how great they were once. I will help you survive.'

'Yes, Sir. Thank you, Sir.'

'You know why? Because I love you.'

Tirenje looked down at her fingers which she was interweaving, bending and stretching out.

'You are no more just a schoolgirl, Tirenje. You are a woman now. You need a man.'

Something in her gave in. Something in me thumped and quivered as soon as I had uttered the last words. Like when you sit on a platform at a political meeting, waiting your turn to speak; and then after your mind has taken a trip somewhere else you suddenly remember that it will soon be your turn to speak. Thump! the heart goes. And you're left quivering inside. In that state, as I sat on the bed, I had, with the words *you need a man*, marked the end of one phase and the beginning of another. I might as well have given myself a rude reminder that the audience would soon be listening to me.

I thought I felt something in her either reaching out for me or opening up for me to enter, or both. Something powerfully elemental was burning, twisting and pushing up against the frontiers of decorum that had been established for both of us. I held her hands in my left one. The right caressed her breasts. Without wanting to resist she struggled. With one deep sigh, as of one crying for help — not to be saved, but to be able to contain the ecstasy — with that one long sigh she yielded . . .

Tirenje often teased me whenever we made love after this. 'You overpower me like *nsato*,' she would say. 'You hold me as if you were never going to let me go, like a python, as if you were going to eat me up alive.' And I would laugh. The thought of being compared to *nsato* was flattering as well as funny.

Two years later Tirenje finished junior secondary school. She was nineteen — closer to twenty. I had just returned from seeing her and her people at Musoro when I found a note waiting for me under the door. Musoro is a little farming town south of Chipata on the Malawi border, very near the Seventh Day Adventist Mission station where I went for teacher training. The note told me the Superintendent of the school wanted to see me in his office first thing the next day. That night I thought very much about the python. Why that particular night I could not understand. Perhaps it was because Tirenje's mother was wasting away so wretchedly, and her body, as I had seen it that weekend, gave me a shock I had not experienced before. It looked like a log that had been vomited by the river on its banks. Like nothing that suggested life. Tirenje's story was that her mother had never outgrown the shock she had sustained the day both of them saw a python constrict a goat. She had fallen seriously ill.

'It has just been growing worse and worse,' Tirenje said to me the first time I visited Musoro with her. 'Father keeps trying one herb after another, one doctor follows upon the heels of another, rattles and scatters bones to divine the disease, leaves his herbs.' ('And the journey stretches out,' I thought.) 'Like when people keep telling you you do not have far to walk, it's just over this hump or that hill and you do not seem to be getting anywhere.' That was how she summed it up.

I had learned a lot about the ways of the python when I was a boy. Almost every adventurous boy in our area — anywhere in Central Africa — sooner or later meets with *nsato*. Or more exactly, finds him. For he is king of his territory. Fangs, none, but sharp teeth, yes; fights only when wounded or attacked; seldom wants human flesh, only if he has gone mad; surrounds the eggs to incubate them. That is what our elders often told us. The day I saw the king, he scared me almost out of my mind. You never want to see him again. All you need to know is that he lives in the neighbourhood. I thought that night: how come a creature like that can look after its eggs and, soon as they hatch, each of the children takes his own way immediately? Just as if they were at kindergarten school and were going back to different homes? It occurred to me that while the idea of the python gave me a glimpse into the externals of power, to Tirenje it meant something to be apprehensive about, something you think of only as a potential molester . . .

'I want to see him again,' Tirenje said, with a strange tone in her voice.

'Whatever for?' I asked, not a little puzzled.

'Just to see him again, so that I can understand what it is he thinks of doing when he sees me, and what I think I want to do when I see him. I want to know if I can trust him.'

'Not if *he* can trust *you*?'

'You are trying to mix up my thinking.'

'He is a king. A real king doesn't go about picking fights with small creatures like human beings.'

Nsato, nsato, I whispered as I fell asleep. Deep and sound.

'Have you anything to tell me, Mr Chirundu?' The superintendent went straight to the point. There were always more pleasing sights than his face. But this morning he seemed to have an invisible whip in his hand. His face always looked windswept. One of those that seem to tell you all the sufferings of mankind, the doom that awaits it, the futility of any efforts to avoid it, including Noah Hackett's own doom. And yet he had eyes that never seemed to look at you straight. When his face was directly in your line of vision, all you saw was a glaze over the eyes. At first, I found it unsettling to talk to him. It seemed my words were bouncing back off a wall, with his eyes looking in that fashion. Sometimes I imagined his head would soon sway from side to side before he struck. Like a snake trying to focus because its eyes see sideways.

'Tell you anything — like what, Mr Hackett?'

'I have a letter from Preacher Maunda of Musoro Baptist Church.'

About Tirenje, I thought. I said nothing.

After a deep breath: 'Here, read it.'

I thought I saw a leer on his lips that seemed to say, *I've got you. You can't deny it. I've no mercy for people who live in sin.* Yes, the letter told Hackett that Tirenje was pregnant. He said I had done it and neither she nor her father felt bad about it. It ended: 'I think iti isi goode for you to no dis bicoss Mistere Chimba isi oni you stuff ende we

17

are Christ bruthers. Dis isi against the testamint of our Lodi Jesus, dis gels child bon in sin when he bon ende no marij. Amen. Your insyde the Lod.'

'Bloody pastoral illiterates!' I said breathlessly. 'Why can't they mind their own business?'

'It's the pastor's business,' Hackett put in. 'It concerns the morals of his flock, and I'm concerned with the morals of the school. Surely you can't be so dim as not to see the connection?'

'You can make it your business if you want, as long as you don't expect me to acknowledge your role in the matter.'

'Let's get this thing straight, are you going to marry the girl?'

'You mean the *lady?*'

'*Are* you going to marry her?'

'Yes and no.'

'Mr Chirundu, this is a serious matter.'

'So the conference of birds must have said when they hauled up the owl to accuse him of going about at night and sleeping in day-time. Slightly irregular, do the English not say?'

He just looked at me. Which was fine, as he normally didn't allow one to come in. Certainly not in a discussion. When he wanted answers, yes. And if your answer was evasive, he just looked at you. As if he had spent hours rehearsing his questions, so that if an answer or two came to him offside, as we say in soccer, he was thrown off balance. I waded in.

'Let me make things easy for you, Mr Superintendent. *You* brought the subject up, not me, and I don't feel obliged to answer your questions. I now oblige because I want to get it over with and I don't like to feel as if I'm on trial. Miss Tirenje Mirimba is a woman I'm in love with. She is going to have my baby. Understand? *My* child. Whether or not I'm going to marry her is no one's business outside our families.'

'Sin, abject sin, damnation!' he hissed.

'I haven't finished. I have seen your church, Baptist, Methodist, Presbyterian, Anglican, Roman, kick our people around on charges of so-called immorality. I've seen you English and American missionaries hound our teachers because they made their women colleagues pregnant, or any woman for that matter, before marriage. You have denounced them publicly, driven them out of your schools, made it impossible for them to find work in any other institution. I've seen you force teachers to marry simply to cover up premarital pregnancy and make it look decent. Crash landing, we call it! You terrorize teachers

18

this way because you know teaching jobs are scarce. And then when the marriage can't last, you refuse to acknowledge a divorce – the only sensible solution in the circumstances. Yes, I have seen you gloat and fume over reports by members of the community who come to tell you their daughter – no matter how old – has been made pregnant by one of your teachers. I've seen you march against a teacher and drive him into the wilderness virtually, demoralize him simply because he had a little fun and a child was on the way – a child he wasn't denying anyhow. I've seen you missionaries hold court and conduct a witch hunt to seek out the scapegoat where the headmaster or principal or even one in your position was your billy goat. I've been at teachers' meetings where white inspectors came to address us and all they did was harangue and threaten us for making school girls and mistresses pregnant – 'low morals' you call it, don't you? What kind of –'

'You've spoken enough, there's –'

'Let me finish! I know I'll never have an opportunity to tell you what I think of this stinking business. I want to tell you this. We've one privately owned pharmacy within a radius of not less than fifty miles. Your clinic would never dream of selling rubber sheaths which are the only prophylactic in this country. The Copperbelt is full of them because there are many white people living there. Do you know anything about the sex life of an African? Do you care to know? Waiting breathlessly every month to see if she was going to get her period, waiting breathlessly when she doesn't. You leave the sperm –'

'I'm not going to sit and listen to this filthy talk!'

'Yes you are, Mr Superintendent. How can you justify mission schools if those who run them are too self-righteous to listen to those they are supposed to uplift?'

'If we didn't build schools the government would not, you'd still be in the bush.'

'That's not the point. We didn't call you. Once you *had* come and your salvation was assured in heaven because of your work here, don't you think *we* ought to judge whether you're humane or not? You should know the money the colonial government pays you and the teachers comes from our sweat and labour in the copper mines. What your church overseas sends you is blood money. The English people have been kept in comfort and wealth because of the raw materials they have been carting out of African soil – oh, why all this tedious talk? You took me off the track. I was saying you leave the sperm in there and take your chances or you retreat before you arrive or you use the stupid rubber bag. Have you ever looked at your own sperm in a bag, Mr Hackett? Hideous! Ah, I can see Mr Hackett is uneasy. You think I'm the personification of all the sins of the flesh, don't you?'

I realised that I had not sat down at all throughout my little speech. He had not offered me a seat. I could have taken any chair, but I was not in the mood for comfort. I remember how recklessly confident I felt as I went on. How measured my breathing was towards the end.

'I used to worry that much, then I said to myself, I said, "Chimba, why do you fear shadows? These strangers will be gone one day. Even if they stay on, they won't be standing at the gate jingling their keys and demanding that you tell them your Christian name." I don't care anymore what happens because I love Miss Mirimba and nobody's going to make me marry her before I decide. I may just decide I don't want to marry her even though I love her. What kind of God is yours that doesn't seem to love people who love each other unless they rush into marriage vows? Does it displease Him when people love each other so much that marriage vows seem trivial? *Your* people — *your* people, Mr Hackett — in Europe — they sleep with women they'll never marry and marry women they may never sleep with except when they want to make a child. We had polygamy on this continent and then you come and tell us it's anti-Christian. Your people can splice any woman as often as they like and keep mistresses and we're told it's a sin to have a concubine. I've finished.'

I felt as if Mr Hackett had come to *me* for a scolding instead of the other way round. I felt I had diminished him. 'Let's bury the Hackett!' was our slogan whenever we toasted — we his teachers — among ourselves. And when we stumbled out into the dark after a bout, making our way home, we shouted 'Let's bury the Hackett!' And I knew he was not the kind that could bury anything but a corpse. A wounded man is like a wounded leopard: mean and dirty.

'I've been more patient than I had intended to be, so God help me,' he said dryly.

'You *had* to be patient. Don't you people pray God to give you patience? And yet you're so used to waving doctrine in the face of challenge. You know yourself you couldn't advance a logical argument to counter the common facts of everyday life. What's more: I'll even decide *when* my penalty is to begin.'

'I give you twenty-four hours to leave the school,' Hackett said with all the authority he could summon up. His neck, the colour and texture of a turkey's, seemed to shrink back into human shape as he made his pronouncement. His Adam's apple quivered. 'I regard this as a misde-meanour. You know the regulations.' The Adam's apple quivered again.

'My bond agreement says I should serve a minimum of five years, I've done four. You know there are better schools I'd rather have been teaching at but for the same stinking moral code. But it couldn't be worse than teaching under a Hackett. On principle I'll complete my bond period — next year.'

'For the good of your soul may God forgive your profanity and in-sults. We're charitable and can let you go now.'

I hated that appearance of humility behind which I knew there was no warmth. The wounded leopard . . . And I hate people who try to saunter out of their element. Like those dehydrated hippos that have wandered too far from the river and begin to act queer. Hackett was clearly out of his element, but then I had blocked his return route, back to his pool. Now he was looking ridiculous.

I lost my temper again. I said, 'Don't rush me, Mr Hackett, don't rush me. I must earn money for my child's clothing and food. Miss Mirimba's father's getting on in years and his garden doesn't yield as much as it used to. I've got all of 1959 ahead of me. Being in your school is no picnic, in fact I wish I had made a schoolgirl pregnant. Then you could dismiss me for misdemeanour in the real official sense — with twenty-four hours' notice.'

He stood there, dumbstruck, but in a posture that suggested all kinds of sinister intentions.

April 1, evening

They never met to speak to each other, of course, Tirenje and Monde. Tirenje kept up that look of calm and self-confidence mixed with pain-ful contemplation. Although I had hoped to see her outside the court, I didn't want to talk to her. After all I regarded her as a club in the Prose-cutor's hand to castigate me with, whatever joy he found in it, as he ad-mitted. I know she will not make any attempt to meet me. Why should she? Monde took the stand this afternoon. By sheer force of habit, I read the proceedings in *Capricorn's* Letters to the Editor, too, still plug-ging the idea of my suspension. I work at the Ministry three hours in the morning before court, and three hours after, 4 to 7 p.m. There's this cursed strike hanging over our heads. Or should I say *my* head?

The next witness: Monde Chirundu, née Lundia. She told the court how I had first suggested we marry by Bemba customary law. How she objected to this. How we then registered the marriage under the Ordinance. She told those servants of the law how she had asked if I had divorced Tirenje. Said I told her I knew what I was doing. By my grandfather's living spirit! What did Monde take this to mean, the court wanted to know. That I knew the law, that I had read books (in her own words).

Clare, my counsel, continues to play the game. Che Chimimba, the Prosecutor, in his fat pomp, taking himself seriously, wielding his position, clubbing a man who's down for a while . . . Careful, heavyweight, a wounded leopard is a dangerous beast! I had told Monde that we had married by customary law, Tirenje and I. And a long separation such as ours — four years — was as good as a divorce. Of course I only explained to her after the summons that I had not told her the whole truth. 'Don't worry,' she said in her sophisticated way. 'I'm your rightful wife. You can still get a proper divorce and I'll wait for you.' As if she knew that was just what I had thought of. Women! Except that this was not the route I had mapped out. Whenever she had brought up the subject again, in that way a woman has who is happy but wants to see if she can be sad, I was impatient. This she told my advocate. Why did you think he knew the law? the Prosecutor asked. Because he knows a lot, he is an educated man, he has read books, he is a Government man, a big man . . .

Well done, Monde, just what I had told you to say. She was exhausted after the day. I thought she would say something about Tirenje. No. I didn't ask her either. I found her sitting languidly on the sofa. I fixed her a martini. Leaning back like that, she looked seductive.

Oh, there was that ancient registrar also who came to give evidence. Simply that he has a record to show that Tirenje and I were married by him in 1959. Exhibit G. He warned us that day that the Ordinance marriage superseded the traditional rites, recorded or not.

Mutumba announces dinner.

Monde goes upstairs to bed. Later I follow. However exhausted, she's always ready. Easy to trigger off. She will moan and gasp at the first touch, almost swamp you with her eagerness. Every movement of hers in the house, any time of day, seems to say to you, 'Come in, it's moist and vibrating for you.' Anywhere, in the kitchen, bathroom, in the middle of the lounge — anywhere. Moves with power, too, considering her slender form. Surrenders to the point of almost dissolving in you. Tirenje — now *that's* another proposition altogether. She doesn't rush you, won't be rushed herself. Wants you to earn it, almost. Often makes a fight of it. But when she is ready to be conquered, she will lie there, waiting to ferry you across. She won't hug you, finger your tools as Monde does: she's too bashful for that. But her whole body will heave against you, make you really feel it's yours to possess. She'll ferry you across, yelling without any inhibition. That way you feel spontaneously that you should also vocalize your movements, your arrival. Between them, it would, if I had not stayed so long from Tirenje, give the two sides of me a needed outlet . . .

I have big things to think about tonight. The strike. Tomorrow night I have to report on it to the Cabinet. Two weeks before the trial we reached a deadlock, the government and the Government Transport Workers Union. As I make my way downstairs, my nephew, Moyo, is standing in the lounge waiting for me. I find it difficult to think of him as my nephew. Just now I see him primarily as a member of the executive of the Transport Workers Union.

'Greetings, asibweni!' he says, standing up. Some days, like now, he says *asibweni* as any person might call an older man 'uncle', rather than as a blood relation.

'Greetings, Moyo!' He stands five feet tall, maybe three inches more. His facial skin clings close to the bone, which gives him a look of being ten years older than his twenty-two. He has an air of arrogance or self-confidence I detest in boys his age. Arrogance sits easier on the shoulders of ripe adulthood. But then I never really knew my nephew before he arrived in the capital with his grandfather, almost three years ago. I had seen him as a little boy whenever I visited my sister — his mother. So I resent him for what he has turned into now without being able to say I may be wrong, considering his upbringing et cetera, et cetera. I resent him. He is one of the young men who gave the transport workers' organization a new life. It had been formed under the colonial government. When independence came, corruption, apathy, lack of leadership had rendered it dormant. Once revived, it was a union to reckon with — a body 3 000 strong, consisting of all drivers of government cars, trucks, tractors.

'Is this official or social?' I asked impatiently.

'I thought you might hear what my executive says about the strike.'

My executive, he says — the upstart!

'Yes?'

'The strike will be postponed until your case is over, asibweni.'

'And then?'

'Whichever way the scales go, we'll go on strike.'

'This is absurd, Moyo! *You* among my enemies!'

'But asibweni, the strike is against the authorities, not asibweni personally!'

I trembled as I said, 'It's the same. Why would your union decide on this moment when my hands are tied behind my back? Is that manliness?'

'That's exactly what I've come about, asibweni. The secretary of the union missed you by a few minutes at the Ministry so I offered to bring the letter telling you of the latest decision.'

Telling you! Who are you to tell me anything? Abusing trade union privilege, eh!

'Tell me.' I am impatient with this herdboy come to the city.

'The executive says that it will postpone the strike until the trial is over.'

'No matter what the outcome?'

'No matter what the outcome.'

'Surely you haven't come all this way from Kabwata to tell me this?'

'Asibweni, it is about Aunt Tirenje — er —'

'What about her? I don't want to see her!' *What am I saying? I do want to see her but I don't want to take the initiative.*

'She does not want to see you, asibweni. Or perhaps she *does* want to, only — only — perhaps she does not want to listen to the language of her heart. It is me, asibweni. It is like this: the elders teach that we must talk. We must talk among ourselves. Talk cleanses and frees the heart, it heals a lot of aches. It helps the boil to burst.'

The small man's voice is trembling. Must have rehearsed this pastoral speech several times on the way here.

'Who should talk?'

'Asibweni and Aunt Tirenje and myself and her cousin in Libala township, we can meet and talk. A woman must have people, people to talk to, people of her own blood or people she knows. A person without people is lost, her mind may break and she may bring sorrow upon us one day. It is I who am afraid, asibweni.'

This twit — so full of himself, gods of my fathers!

'There's a trial on, Moyo.'

'That is the white man's way, we have our own ways. Even after the trial, asibweni and auntie will have to decide whether they can continue as man and wife.'

24

The damn cheek he has! 'Will you concern yourself with things fitting for your age!'

'Sorry, asibweni, I did not mean to offend you.'

The little man is sitting with his body bent forward as if he has stomach ache. He has funny square shoulders that always give the impression of a man trying to keep his ego afloat. Bending forward like that seems to diminish the effect of the shoulder-pushing act. There's something touching about it. It disturbs me to find myself in opposition when nothing but pity is possible in my attitude towards weaklings. Yet this is the one time when I'd like to pity Moyo and Tirenje. Maybe because they threaten me. Yesterday they were weak and helpless and simpler to understand. Today they are complicated, they are in a position to wield power. And largely because they have each enlisted the support of others, they virtually broke into the arsenal and grabbed the weapons with which to threaten me — the labour union and the white man's law. Tirenje is staying with Moyo, and the thought that they are comparing notes and ideas on how to destroy me is a spear hanging from my side.

Furiously I say, 'I gave her money after she came to the city, you're my witness, she returned it, what kind of pride is that? Look, Moyo, take this money and buy food for both of you. You needn't tell her about it.'

I whip out five kwacha notes and hold them toward him. He takes them. 'Only for her sake,' he says, standing up. As he makes towards the door, I say impetuously, 'Moyo, take an uncle's caution: you're playing with fire, playing around with trade unions the way you do.'

'I don't consider this as a game, asibweni.'

Those square shoulders again, that arrogant smile!

'You're a newcomer in this, and you could get hurt, badly hurt. You're running full tilt against authority, you're not old enough to bear the consequences. A mere twenty-two-year-old cub like you getting mixed up in strikes. Get out of the committee and just be one of the rank and file. That way you can't stick your neck out.'

'Did asibweni caution himself like this when he was in the teachers' organization? Would he respect me as a man if I followed the advice?'

I'm wondering at this time why I thought it fit to warn Moyo. I can't explain the reason. Is it because of a blood relationship? True, I would have thought it unmanly to quit a labour union. 'But we were fighting a colonial administration,' I reply. 'Today it's like carrying knives against your own government, led by the same party that got you out of bondage. You're denying the government a fair chance to straighten out things, to provide more hospitals and clinics, more schools, revise wage systems and so on. The worst thing that could have happened to you was to meet that South African agitator. This country's ruled by black people, theirs by white people. How can our people strive for improvements with the same weapons South Africans use? Don't you see the stupidity of this, Moyo? We don't need a workers' revolution here, man. It's all right in South Africa where they're oppressed. You're not oppressed here, you've got your own government that is building a nation and organizing its economic resources. Leave all this foolishness, these trade union slogans are stupid. Organize a union and negotiate peacefully. You can still call off the strike and the public will realize you've done a noble thing.'

Moyo stares at me. I shall never forget that small face under the light in the porch. I cannot fathom it. Wonder, incredulity, contempt, sadness, pity, seem all to converge in that expression on his face.

I pour myself a Scotch and sit on my favourite chair.

My mind seems to vibrate with the sound of my own words after he has disappeared quietly into the shadows of my yard. Studs Letanka. The sound of the name gives me heartburn. Moyo was a simple innocent country boy when he came here. In two years I can't recognize him anymore. Eighteen months in that College of Public Education and trade union teaching have messed him up. How many times have I warned him! Told him to build himself up and get a better job, more respectable ... Those refugees in jail. People like Studs ... ought to be locked up with the refugees. They come here without any freedom organization to speak for them. How can we tell they're not spies! They'd be dangerous as long as they were outside. That Studs! But no one can touch him ... Can't touch an employee of the International Technical Education or we'll have the African Economic Unity flying in any moment. Damn it, with my hands tied behind my back and Wanika glowering at me, I feel like an invalid strapped to a wheel chair. I know I could be more than a match for these skittish young donkeys. I'd teach them to respect their superiors. Our people need a tough hand ... democratic rule doesn't work, they can't manage such a principle, they're waiting to be led or misled ... As things are, I must let things take their course, for better or for worse. I'll get them eventually. I was destined for great things.

As I lie in bed beside Monde, feeling cosy against her warm flesh, Moyo's words about Tirenje and me living together again echo rudely in my mind. Why have I never applied my mind to that proposition? Do I still love her? Do I want to bring her to the city as my wife? I love her. But I won't be forced into an either-or position. More than once I begged Tirenje to come to the city. I would house her and the children separately from Monde. I asked her father to plead with her. 'I cannot do such a thing, my son,' was all he said. 'This thing you are asking her to do, it is too big. I do not want her to do anything like it simply because her father asked it. I am not even sure myself whether you are doing the right thing by keeping two wives — the right thing by the three of you.'

I decided I was just not going to think about it, to let it bother me. I think it amounts to this: I love Tirenje as much as I love Monde. I resent the idea that I should have to make a choice: if you love both women, make up your mind which one you're going to live with! Inanity — why should I have to put up with it?

Tonight it's like a spirit come from the land of unborn decisions, secret longings, unappeased resentments, half-answered questions, to haunt me. After this, she'll be foolish to refuse me a divorce. And yet something tells me she might just make it impossible for me to carry on with Monde even while she knows she does not want me. She *can't* want me back. She doesn't behave like a woman out in search of her man, to wrench him from the arms of a city woman. But of course Monde is not a city whore, nor am I living a debauched life. I'm a big man, a responsible man, a public servant!

What a first day of April!

The weekend following upon my talk with Mr Hackett, Superintendent of the Seventh Day Adventist Mission, I took a bus to visit my father in Shimoni.

'*There's* your Seventh Day Adventist!' I said after my recital of the Hackett meeting. The sense of moral triumph I had felt over Hackett and all that he represented had worn off to almost a sense of weariness. But my resolve had not weakened at all.

'If you do not deny this child,' father said, his eyes fixed on the ground, 'I mean if you do not deny it, why not just marry the girl?' He chuckled mirthlessly. 'I mean — you just love to quarrel even where nothing calls for it.'

'Should I marry simply because Tirenje's going to have a child?'

'What else are you planning to do?'

'I just want to take my time. There's no hurry.' I didn't want to tell him that Tirenje did not like to be one of two or three wives. Because that was not the only bothersome thing. What I had seen go on in the church, in its missions, had hardened me to the point where I didn't think it worthwhile to do anything that might amount to surrender to their religious inanities. 'Besides, it was never a crime among our people to have a child before you marry. I've not committed any sin.'

'My son! My own child — to say things like this!' Father shook his head which was covered with grains of gray hair. 'In my seventieth year I never thought I would hear my own son say such things — child of my own loins!'

'Look at it up or down the road, father: if it is a sin to make a woman pregnant, then it must have been a sin to sleep with her in the first place. If she did not become pregnant, is the sin of sleeping with her wiped out? Evidently in your eyes — in the eyes of these squinting missionaries — it would not have mattered if there had been no pregnancy, as long as they didn't know the two were sleeping together before marriage. Without pregnancy, how would they know I was sleeping with the girl?'

'It would still be on your conscience and it is you, not the church that would be damned.'

'I will not argue about that. Being damned or being saved is something like the stories about giants and spirits we entertain children with. Who can know who is damned, who is saved?'

'What has happened to you since you became a teacher?' His voice was high-pitched this time. He was literally shaking all over. 'I mean to say what happened? What kind of monster, devil's messenger do I see before me? Is this what you have been teaching at school?'

'I could not do that and still keep my job. I've been lying and lying to those poor children until I almost believed in the scriptures. I was teaching myself in the process.'

'The Superintendent was guided by the hand of God to dismiss you. You get to smell out evil when you are in constant touch with God.'

'You know what is wrong with you, father? We are now in 1958. I am twenty-six, you have been a convert for only twenty years. You were baptized just before I was — when I was six. Before that you had lived as a non-Christian for fifty years. Put fifty years against twenty, if you see what I mean. So you have swallowed everything — mountains and antheaps — everything you were taught. But can you really forget fifty years of life — all that the elders taught? I see you walk about and say Christian things. But I know your mind is not in what you are saying.

'Do not go too far, young man! Do not go too far, you hear me!'

My father seemed to bend under my sickle as it were. Then he straightened up and said, 'And you! Are you saying what is really in your heart and mind? Or are you repeating somebody else's words?'

I hesitated. 'Of course I'm speaking my mind.' Even as I uttered the words I knew I was evading the question. How much of what a man says can he claim to be native to himself, how much is the product of someone else's teaching? We are taught things, but surely as we turn them over in our minds we give them our own stamp. This much I learned when I was training as a teacher. One tends also to remember a treasure of things said by people one admired. Like Hugh Corkery, my Irish teacher in Principles of Education. One of that rare breed of Europeans who take their vocation in Africa seriously without being overbearing. Not as a teacher, who has brought light to bush communities, but as one who was ready to listen to his students, to learn from them.

'Don't be fooled,' Corkery would say, 'by all these ideas Europe has continually been dumping in Africa. Europe has no use for them . . . They are bleached ideas and Europeans are trying to revive their own faith by transplanting it onto African soil, to see if it will germinate and justify their own sense of power, of superiority. Don't even trust *me.*'

I remembered his words so vividly. He urged us to use the school for the tools it could afford us . . . learn new things, learn how to seize power and to hold on to it . . . not to forsake our ancestors for something Europeans were themselves throwing out on the dung heap. 'If I were to run an educational system on this continent,' Corkery said, 'I'd begin where your elders left off, and I would be guided by their wisdom in deciding what to put into a curriculum. I would stress human relations all the way. But even then I should constantly test my judgment. It is not my function to tell Africans what to do. I am also a selfish man, I came out here to extend myself. But once being here I tremble, as if I were in the presence of an oracle. That oracle is you put together in front of me. I now realize all the more what a perilous thing it is when you undertake to teach those outside your own culture.'

And how perilous! That man made us realize how perilous was the journey, from the time one's mind opened up to the scores of possibilities and avenues and expectations. We would forever be making choices or failing to make them; we would forever be walking the often tightrope narrow path between what is elevating and exciting for ourselves as individuals in the acquisition of this new power and what is beneficial for the community, materially and spiritually . . .

That man's words sank deep into me in a way no other man's teaching had ever done. Although my political life was later to claim all my mind, all my senses, practically all my feelings, somewhere in some deep cool recess of my being I heard something like whispers, like muted rumblings, like a voice of caution, like rebellion, like some ancestral incantation, like the voice of an elder trying to shout across the torrential waterfall or a swollen boulder-heaving river. The noise of politics threatened always to shut off that recess, seal it forever. And I deliberately lost myself in that din so that nothing might slow me down. And the political arena became the element in which I thrived most.

But all this was to be later. The Irishman had sown the seed, and now dialogue was becoming more and more difficult between me and my father. The Hackett incident had only pushed me into the first phase of a realization that my father and I were drifting farther apart.

'Our ancestors would not have allowed a man to drink out of a calabash before asking for it in the proper way. This —'

'Let the girl's parents claim their rights then,' I cut in. 'The church should stay out. You could still sleep with a girl in your days as long as you took care not to leave your seed in her. If you did, you were not driven out into the wilderness and made to feel as if you had killed a man or slept with your own sister.'

His face twitched like that of a man who has blundered into a spider's web and is trying to tear off the strands.

'Stubborn, self-willed!' my father muttered. 'I can smell the blood of a Chirundu inside there. Nothing could ever subdue the blood of a Chirundu. You need a little humility. In my old age I know now this is what we always needed.'

The next time we ever spoke at length, it was my father who did all the talking. He delivered a tirade. That was a few months before Tirenje moved against me. When we spoke at Shimoni after my confrontation with Hackett, it became more evident than ever before what his conversion had done to him. And yet I thought I sensed in the tone of his voice, when he talked about humility, a touch of regret and helpless attachment to a thing that had beaten down the fire in him to a mere smoulder. Or was it just age? I could not tell. The legend he seemed to hold on to about the fierce blood of the Chirundus referred more accurately to the direct line that came from my grandfather through my own father to me. Something tragic happened that started with my grandfather's brother and continued through my father's cousin. The Bemba are notorious for in-breeding. My grandfather simply refused to marry his blood cousin and prevailed upon my father to resist the temptation to take one or more of the many women who were in one way or another related to him biologically. 'Get this baggage out of the house as soon as they have swept the homestead!' grandfather could be heard shouting to his wives. The 'baggage' would be the women, all relatives in one degree or another, who, my father related, were always hovering about hoping he would add one of them to his homestead.

I had read a bit of genetics as an extra-curricular activity in teacher training. From discussion with the German district surgeon who came once a week to talk to us on the subject, I got a picture of the horrors of in-breeding my bowels could hardly bear. There were several families which suffered heavy casualties, some more than others. One branch of the Chirundu line was a case in point. It seems to have begun with my great-grandfather's brother who was the issue of another wife in their family. This brother married a blood cousin — a maternal aunt's daughter. From then on, as the circle widened, these people seemed to be irresistibly attracted to one another. There were to be found in the Chirundu family an adult with a monstrously huge head which he had carried since birth; a homicidal maniac; drunks; bums and hoboes; non-starters; petty minds; mental cases and other nameless deviates. My family had its own share of looking after one deviate or another who just seemed to have strayed into our home. Both of my father's wives were goodhearted. They regarded it as a duty assigned them by the ancestors to look after all the people who continued to come and live with us and then leave and disappear into anonymity. 'Where do they stop, just before they die?' I used to ask my father. 'Somewhere,' he'd answer, 'where neither you nor I could ever prepare for their departure from this world. Like animals that roam the wilderness until the earth takes them back.'

I grew up in a home constantly teeming with life. Some of this life was made up of my uncles and aunts and cousins. Debris on a river bank — that is how I must see them now, but in my innocence I considered them normal. They treated me no better or worse than if I were their own child. What I did not like in particular was the number of times they used to send me about to fetch this, do that: water here, snuff there, beer there, when I could be playing or doing my school work in quiet. As I grew up I began to notice a kind of pattern, however vague in my mind. Some of these people slept too much, some drank too much, some grinned vacantly or made childish jokes. If I talked back to any of them my mother or father, whoever was within hearing distance, would give me a clout on the shoulders. These people would all sleep in one room or out in the backyard, while my two mothers each had a room. We had no such things as a dining room or an enclosed kitchen. We ate on the floor. So mealtime looked like some family ceremony.

My father was not often patient with our relatives. Left to himself, he would run them out of the asylum. That's what it looked like at certain periods. When some moved on, others came in. Particularly the drunks and the drones drove my father into fits of rage. One uncle came home from the village drunk and tried to force his way into my other mother's bed, on a night my father was with my own mother. When my father heard a scream, he rushed to the bedroom. He dragged my uncle out, stripped him in the yard and whipped him till he bellowed out loud. Next day my uncle was shown the road. 'Why do the ancestors afflict us like this?' my father would say, almost in a wail.

There was this other man. One of those who grinned like a performing monkey. He would sit in the shade of the bluegum tree at the side of the house, washing his feet and his sandals made out of motorcar tyre. He was always washing his feet. Three times a day, it looked to me. After school I would go to the bluegum tree to make small talk with him. That perpetual grin always gave me the impression of a man who knows it all; who has been there, and what is more, knows what is on the other side of the far-off blue hills — where he is going.

'Do not let them fox you,' he would say.

'Who?'

'Them.' He would look down into the tub of water. As if the answer lay there.

'They drove me out of my lands,' he said, underlining the statement with his grin, which by now had become much like one of the organs of his face.

'Who did that?' I tried again.

'This time they will never get me right. They will never drive me out of my lands.'

'Which lands?'

'All this.' With the sweep of his hand he indicated the whole earth. 'I can stay anywhere, I can die anywhere.'

And that grin, those wasted eyes, spelt irredeemable failure.

'What lands did he mean, Papa?'

My father laughed heartily, which he seldom did where his relatives were concerned. 'What lands? What lands indeed! An ant has more terri-

tory for its nest than he could ever possess.' Locking his jaws to accentu-
ate disgust and sorrow and rebellion he said, 'Failures, weaklings,
wrecks, dead lumber! How can they escape punishment after they
have all been to the same well and drained it. Beware, Chimba, never
marry a blood relation. You can see the workings of the curse yourself.'

And that was before I read genetics. For a long time I was scared lest
my children should turn out to be a throwback to something that might
have found its way into our branch of the Chirundu tree. Both my
father and I were glad of the possibility of looking in another ethnic direction for a wife. He himself had married outside, for better or for
worse.

My father married a pretty woman. Much later, I thought, than I
would have liked to marry. He did not think so. He had been a restless
young man. In his middle twenties, just before World War I broke out,
he was in Nyasaland. He had just walked there with two of his friends
in search of something he could not describe. There was the drought, of
course, for one thing. One of the worst the land could ever remember.
Some people retraced their steps to the Congo, where the Bemba and
Lunda had originally come from. Some people drifted south, others
went into Angola. People who had spilled over the border from Nyasaland in the early days of the century tried to dissuade my father and his
friends. They spoke of frequent droughts, lack of land, *chifwamba* —
the Yao and Arab raiders who wanted slaves for the east-coast trade.
But Chirundu and his friends went anyhow. They were shown where
Zwangendaba's trail of fire and blood had gone through. Zwangendaba
who, in the 1830s and 1840s, led his Ngoni people out of the Zulu
nation and trekked north into Nyasaland. A man who supplanted and
scattered kingdoms wherever he went, including those of Nyasaland.
The young men worked on the boats on Lake Nyasa, then on white
people's farms. One day in 1915 they heard of John Chilembwe's
one-day uprising against the English, in which he tried to invoke the
Christian doctrine to instigate revolution.

After seven years my father returned, at the age of thirty-seven.
Alone. He gave a woman a child among the Bisa people and married her
four years later. By this time he had become aware of the evils of in-
breeding. The child who was later to become Moyo's mother turned out
to be the only one his wife was going to give him. When they found
they could have no more children, he took a second wife, much younger than he — my mother. She was of the Lunda who had ancient ties

33

with the Bemba. Three sons were born to them. My brothers are still alive. As soon as the sons reached an age when they wanted to be independent, they left, to set up their own homes. Several people considered my father such a hard man that the rumour went the rounds that even his own children couldn't bear him. He was little more than a reptile, whose children take their own ways as soon as they see the light of day. No family life. But of course this was an exaggeration: we *did* have family life. And public opinion meant little to my father, until that crucial turning point came in his life — his conversion to Christianity. He still had strong prejudices against certain tribes, even though he was prepared to marry outside the Bemba people. The Tumbuka people for instance. They were knocked about and enslaved and knocked about by Zwengendaba's Ngoni in Nyasaland. The Bemba and Lunda enslaved Tumbuka this side of the Nyasaland border. 'What kind of people are these!' my father would exclaim. 'Trampled upon by anyone who comes along. They are no longer slaves now but they act like oxen that walk with their heads down even when the yoke has been removed. No spine, no will of their own. Surrounded in a canoe by crocodiles Tumbuka will kill them with his fart.'

Once he had marked them in those terms, he swore that no daughter of his would ever be wife of a Tumbuka. 'When I am deep down in my grave, yes, my sons can marry who they will, I shall have no power to stop them.'

'You do not feel for Tumbuka for having been chased about by stronger people?' I would ask my father. 'Look at the way the white man whittled down the power of our kings. Our Chitimukulu, to give you an illustration. What became of him? How much king was left in him when they had done with him? The white man was not even as fierce as Bemba and Ngoni. In their own way they crush our kings.'

To this he just snorted and turned his face the other way.

A challenge came. One of a small community of Tumbuka living about ten miles north of Shimoni got to know my sister. I was only ten, but I was aware even then of my father's prejudices against Tumbuka, which were common talk in the villages. My sister was insistent. She simply went to her man. His aged father brought the bride price. My father left no room for customary ceremony, made no pretences to be hospitable generally. I was later to learn in my adult years how painful, often humiliating, it is when you discover the extent to which you took it for granted that the private code you live by is also other people's, and the stupidity of such an assumption stares at you pitilessly. My father never, to the best of my knowledge, visited his daughter. My sister came often to bring her children for him to see, to appease the ancestors. When she lost her first daughter she came to Shimoni to confront him with the question, 'Papa, have you asked the ancestors of Chirundu to avenge the wound you inflicted on yourself?'

'I am not a heathen!' my father replied abruptly and passionately.

'Then what is it? I lost my child because you never came to see us to bless our house in Bisa.'

'It is not in my power to bless or curse anybody! It is Jehovah's will.'

'What about the ancestors of the house of Chirundu? What are they to think about the things that are in your heart?'

'That is the path Jehovah has chosen for me.'

'Yes, of course, I am not the first one to be thrown away because of Jehovah, am I? You threw my mother away when Jehovah claimed you. Thank the gods, she has a man again and she lives among her own people.'

That was one of the strangest things I had ever seen happen to a man. At fifty the Seventh Day Adventists conquered him. In 1938 they captured him, baptized him and something in him was laid to rest forever, or chained or just killed outright. They told him he could not keep two wives. He abandoned my sister's mother and re-married my mother by Christian rites. My mother and I were baptized the same year. I was six. We were said to be converted, to be cleansed of our sins. Just like that!

Moyo was born and so his sister after him and they thrived. When my sister died in 1964 — at forty-three — I was deeply grieved. Then her husband died a year later. The house of Mutiso had fallen. Old Mutiso, who had brought the bride price on behalf of his son, was too old to sustain the house. Which is what brought Moyo and the old man to the *kapitolo,* the big city.

The life of my own mother with father is another drama painful to recount. After our baptism, he simply became a tyrant. He ruled the house by the Biblical word. He had been tough and fiery before, but it was admirable. Now there was an alien fire in him. And yet it seemed to torture him even while he bandied Bible and hymn book everywhere. He laid down restrictions. He commanded us to pray morning and night, go to three church services every Sunday. Boarding-school discipline had none of the sting and blistering rub my father's had. My mother must have looked like a Hebrew woman, so I imagined. He preached in

35

the villages and had little time for affectionate talk and gesture.

My two brothers went to work in the Copperbelt and sent money to support us. After I had qualified as a teacher I helped maintain our parents. When my brothers married, I became fully responsible for the upkeep of the home. Father towed my mother about on his preaching circuit. Then it happened. 'She simply packed her bundle,' father told me, looking as if everything he had lived for lay in ashes in front of him. 'She just packed and said to me, she said, "It is enough Chirundu, enough that I have borne you three sons. But this kind of life is not for me. My ancestors have not yet forsaken me." You know, she simply said that and left. "I am going back to my people." Those were the words that came out of her very mouth.'

'Are you not going to bring her back?' I asked.

'No. I cannot turn back to my old ways.'

It was my turn to be baffled. So I said nothing. I was simply confused. Although I contemplated the complexity of the human mind, that did not help me solve the riddle of my father.

I went a few times to see my mother in the north-west. She looked as calm and strong as ever. She was comfortable in the care of her relatives. During my years in the civil service, I sent her money. My predecessor as Minister of Transport often visited his people in the north-west and came to give me news of her. In my campaigning days, I was to see much of Moyo's grandmother — my father's first wife — in Bisa.

When we spoke about Tirenje and me and Hackett and the ancestors and the Church, there was a strange interplay on his face between emotions that seemed to suggest *see what I have come to!* on the one hand, and *my faith can move mountains* on the other. Defeat and mindless obstinacy.

My marriage in November of 1959 and my resignation from the Kapiri school, coincided with the political agitation against the federation Britain had imposed on us in 1952. Political leaders were being jailed while Welenskian shrieks carried word across the Zambesi that African nationalism was so much chaff. Without knowing it, I was in it. A grandfather whose face I could only vaguely imagine had prophesied as much. I was emotionally and mentally ready to enter politics. I was destined for great things . . .

We moved to Kapiri, then to Luanshya, right in the Copperbelt. Things were volatile there, people had always been politically alive since the mine workers' strikes of the forties and fifties. My father-in-law refused to come and live with us, even though Tirenje's mother was dead. He was always good to me. Yet I sensed that he had reservations. I could not put my finger on it. Which irritated me. I want words, thoughts, feelings to come out into the open. I can only deal with what I see and feel and hear. Something he would say, something he would imply, something I could see, or thought I saw, cast a shadow over his face. Although these things bothered me, I resolved they were not going to sour my life with Tirenje. As he was always respectful, there could be no occasion for a quarrel. Of this I was glad. I felt easier with him than with my own father.

We registered our marriage under customary law first, in the Copperbelt. Then we registered it under common law — the Ordinance. 'Why both?' Tirenje asked goodhumouredly. 'To make doubly sure,' I said, almost flippantly.

Right from the time I organized a branch of the National Alliance Party, I realized that I would be sent to the Copperbelt. I did not think the president of our party would take me seriously, but I felt the Copperbelt would eventually be my beat. I was only 27. There were a number of old horses around who wanted to take on the African Congress Movement in copper country. Tongila, the leader of the ACM, was a debauched alcoholic. One of those people who don't die easily but don't want to give way for anybody else either, and are no asset to those they lead. A man with a large nose, thick lips, a cocky neck and shoulders, he did much to tie up the mine workers' union with his political movement. Indeed the ACM was predominantly a mine workers' organization. The British administration and the mining companies were tough on the workers. South African whites had been recruited by the hundred, and it was their high expatriate wages that made the companies reluctant to improve the lot of the African worker. Tongila shook the administration and the companies considerably in the forties and fifties. The worker looked at himself as a worker discriminated against because he was African.

But we would have to do something about Tongila and the ACM. Dislodge them. Destroy him. They were secure and cosy in the high esteem mine labour had for them. So they had become stagnant. Any membership would have to be stagnant to continue to sustain Tongila as a leader. He was now fit only for firewood. He had no political philosophy, no view of what kind of society he wanted to see. The sot! He was a mere obstruction. Like one of those small-town mayors who go on for years because the people think outside that position he would be more dangerous.

In three years I was raised to the Central Committee.

'You deserve no less,' the President said. 'Before you came to this district as one of us there was nothing we could call NAP. You've raised the party in the esteem of the people.' Those words flushed my whole body with a warm, gentle current.

How else? The President himself had spoken. President of the National Alliance Party and future President of the country. That was certain to be so. We were a modern party. We were going to dislodge the African Congress Movement from their traditional stronghold — the Copperbelt. The party relied heavily on the mine workers and had not kept up with the times. The people were waiting for a *political* movement. One that would seize political power from the English. For this we would have to suspend action on mine workers' wages. Workers in other industries were worse off anyhow. And we could not reasonably push for better wages just when we were getting into government ourselves.

The President had spoken. My eyes roved round the long table in the board room of the Municipal Hall. The President sounded tougher than he really was. The son of a teacher-preacher from the Lunda people. Deceptively soft eyes oozing compassion. But you knew it was compassion bestowed from a position of power. You could not mistake this when he declared policy. Ah, *there* is *nsato* for you: the python that will only come at you if you bother him or threaten him in his own lair. No, he is no weakling. He does not have to be in the right: he knows how to use power. That is the man for me.

My eyes roved round. Next to the President, on his right, was his Vice. A cantankerous Bemba who walked with a stoop his enemies swore he put on, for show-off. He wore a beard on his triangular face. It gave one the impression that a Cavalier's hat on his head would complete the picture one often saw in reproductions of oil paintings or in history books which talk about Cromwell's times. But without a hat on, the Vice looked like a newborn mouse. The thin hair on his balding head lay back. The receding forehead seemed to want to take the eyebrows and the eyes with it. He looked wiser and deeper than he really was. Some of the things he mouthed about African culture were plain stupid. And yet he seemed to want to be regarded as a spokesman on culture. I wonder why people would rather speak English badly than speak their mother tongue and let *that* be interpreted into the other main languages of our country. We are in the ridiculous position where we keep telling ourselves and the outside world how wonderful we are or how culturally strong we are, but at one and the same time say all these things in a foreign language that is hopelessly inadequate to capture the spirit, the mood of what we would normally express in our own languages. I insisted on speaking Bemba and Nyanja at public meetings and rallies and English only in Central Committee meetings. Today when I am in the South or West provinces I speak Nyanja and a faulty Lozi respectively and have the Nyanja interpreted into Tonga for the south. The Vice was a poor English speaker, but he carried on in that asinine fashion, expressing himself in English. He would come up with some outrageous spoonerisms, such as we used to laugh over so much in teacher training. Secondary school humour is so different from that in teacher training. Of this I was reminded by the Vice's spoonerisms. They were not funny anymore: *I will leave no turn unstoned; this effort campaign; we are coming to the road of the end; the golonial covernment,* and so on. And he would ride confidently on this kind of idiom without ever looking back! Today things are easier for him: his private secretary writes his speeches for him.

My eyes rested on the bright, young, skittish stallion in the person of Ferdinand Musaka. Full of himself, but not for nothing. Because he was perhaps the most intelligent of all of us. There are people you know are superb material for a Cabinet post. Ferdinand was such a person. Like me. I just knew the route to a government position was carved out for me. The rest of the Central Committee were mediocre stuff. Some of them should have been branch organizers and stayed there. The kind that is always rushing about breathlessly, brandishing a newish briefcase — the most popular symbol of office. The kind that listens very closely to instructions from superiors because he cannot think for himself (the gods bless him!). The man who calls instant committee and branch meetings at the most unreasonable and erratic times in order to lay a complaint against a member or to propose some idea that came to him at dawn as he lay in bed, one he is sure sums up his creative genius. The man who is doomed to be a branch organizer all his life because he has no gumption, no will of his own. To survive he has to be all things to all men; must be prepared to eat dung when he is told to. Let him stay there, damn it, and occupy himself with such local subcommittees as entertainment, fund raising, welfare and so on.

There was of course Chief Luleka. The President had decided to co-opt a chief. The people in the rural areas must be made to believe that we had their interests at heart. We knew that they would be feeling nervous about a central authority that would ignore or strip them of their local power. The British had ruled through them. Gave them the detestable title 'chief'. Made them think they still had their traditional power. Now here was a herd of young bulls coming in to take over. They might not respect traditional authority; they read books and had no time for elders. These were reasonable fears. Why would we need to govern through chiefs when we were sons of the soil, right in their midst? Those wicked ACM leaders: they exaggerated the problem, poisoned the minds of the people; told the chiefs that we were out to drive them out or turn them into mere puppets. They, as the ACM, were going to leave them in authority as traditional local rulers. Wicked! Crude bush politics, I called it. They knew they would have to change the chief's position, but they made it sound as if they were humane and we were an educated demolition squad.

So the Central Committee decided to co-opt Chief Luleka. A kind of mascot. A fetish. They kept him happy, he played the game. Couldn't read. His personal secretary read and interpreted for him. He acted like one who understood everything firsthand. Every so often the President said, 'Tell our father Chief Luleka that . . . What does our father think? . . . Of course we know our father here . . .' Things like that. Dry twigs of formality that crackled in the sensitive ear. But they made the chief feel he was one of the family, a senior member at that. I always thought I would ask our culture monger in the Central Committee one day what he thought we should do with chiefs and other local rulers. I never got round to doing it. Maybe out of mere propriety: he is much older than I. But it would have given my wicked intentions some satisfaction.

'Here is our strategy,' the President said in a meeting of the Central Committee. 'We must form a Youth Brigade. Mobilize them, train them to go from door to door, sign up members and give them NAP cards. There are a lot of youngsters roaming the streets, unemployed. This should keep them out of mischief. First lesson in citizenship and patriotism too. Don't you agree?'

We agreed.

'Comrade Chimba Chirundu, you will organize the youth.'

'Yes, Comrade President,' I said, 'I feel honoured.'

'Never mind honour, it often comes cheap. Go to it! Now remember this for all time — you are not to play rough. Understand?'

'Yes, Comrade President.'

'Youth brigades in other countries have simply got out of hand. The young devils go about insulting grownups and raiding villages for Party cards. I shall not tolerate this.'

'Yes, Comrade President.'

'If any complaint ever reaches me about incidents of physical violence or bad language, I'll fire someone and ask questions afterwards.'

'Comrades,' the President continued, casting his eyes over the meeting. 'Comrade Chirundu gave up the teaching profession to devote his time to the Party. For the last three years he has been cultivating the Copperbelt soil and we can see something germinating now. He has given the Copperbelt a new life. From here on victory over ACM is a foregone conclusion. We have been paying him a mere stipend. This is more than any man can be asked to bear. From now on he is on a fixed salary scale. His rent will be paid by the Party too, a car will be provided solely for his use. Comrade secretary, instruct the treasury accordingly, at once.'

Envy beaming large on black faces. False congratulatory noises. I didn't care about them. I could hardly contain my sense of pride and my joy. I took the first bus home from Kitwe to break the news to Tirenje.

A second child – a daughter – had been born in 1960. The image of her mother. A cheerful thing to whom life must have been a kaleidoscope of rainbows. Tirenje taught sewing as an uncertificated teacher in a primary school in Luanshya. She had carried her last pregnancy with admirable stamina, considering that she was teaching every day.

'You must leave the school, Tirenje, now that I have a full-time paying job,' I said, after announcing the latest news.

'Do you really want me to leave?'

'Yes.'

'I like to teach sewing, Chimba. Can I not just work because I like it?'

'There are two children to look after too.'

'Auntie is good with them, my hours are not long.'

Auntie was a woman we asked to come and live with us. There are always middle-aged and older people who need someone to take them in and care for them because their people are scattered about the country or dead. It costs little to feed and clothe them, they are good with children, they lend fullness to a home, and one's duty to the ancestors is fulfilled by such an act.

'All the same I shall not have my wife work in regular employment.'

She looked away and brushed her nose with the back of her hand.

Whenever she did that I knew it was helpless surrender. Whenever she looked down, it was a way of saying *we haven't heard the last of this.* Like the day a suit of mine arrived from London. Times were hard, but I felt I had to order it. 'Eighteen pounds for a suit,' Tirenje exclaimed, her arms hanging limp on her sides. 'My husband!'

'I am a public servant, Tirenje!'

'We could have waited, my man. Your other suits are not anything like rags.'

'Then I will not buy a new suit for a long time.'

She looked down.

I felt bad about what I had done.

The same year our first child came down with malaria. We lost her.

Tirenje took it harder than I. Yes, grief stabbed painfully. But I had other things to cushion me against some of the pain. Children die, I thought philosophically, nations are born. *Kwacha! Wake up, it is a bright new day!* as our slogan went.

The Federation was certainly going to be dismantled. Independence was just three years away. *Kwacha!* The cry resounded from one end of the country to the other.

'Let me do your secretarial work for you, Chimba,' Tirenje said one day.

'I have got help in the branch office. I do not like to see you wear yourself out on work like this.'

'You think I am too stupid or I do not believe in the things you believe in.' She laughed as she said that. But the accusation in that laugh unsettled me.

There had been women heroes in history, like the warrior queen Mma Ntatise of South Africa who led her people from one conquest to another in the 1820s. But I believed firmly that woman's place is with her family, in the house. I wanted to be looked after so that I could function effectively. My children needed constant attention from a mother. I could not see Tirenje messing with political work.

'I will simply do what you direct me to,' she pleaded once more after I had explained to her my feelings on the matter.

'No.'

'And you do not want me to teach either.'

'No. But rather that than political work.'

'You speak as if I wanted to follow you around making speeches.'

'Can't you understand, woman?'

'I understand.'

'Do you want to go back to teach?'

'As an unqualified teacher? No, no! They give you all the jobs the qualified ones do not want. It was good to keep myself busy teaching sewing. My sewing was going rusty anyhow. No, no teaching for me!'

Tirenje never raised her voice even when she felt passionately about something, in approval or revulsion. Her manner, against my loud voice, exasperated me. She sounded like an older sister to a kid brother, and therefore stronger.

'You drive yourself too hard, Chimba,' Tirenje said one say. 'Even a python grows old and weak. It is the man who goes under, not the work. There is always work.'

My house had become by now a regular meeting place. Men and women, old and young, came round any time. Not for anything in particular. I bought a radiogram and had an electrician fit a loudspeaker above the veranda. People flocked round the house to hear the news three times a day. Often Tirenje served them tea, especially the elderly.

Since the day I had said No, she had not brought up the subject of assisting me with paper work again. She continued her old amiable self.

'You do not hold me like a python any longer,' she said teasingly one morning. 'Your mind is too busy with other people, eh?'

I took her with a ferocity that surprised even me. As we lay panting side by side she said, 'That was not a python, it was a leopard!'

Another child was on the way.

About three months before Tirenje teased me I had met Monde in the big city. We had to visit the city in the south frequently for committee meetings and campaigning. She was serving tea at one of these meetings, as one of the administrative secretaries in the Ministry of Commerce and Industries. Tall, slender as a buck. Her eyes were narrow, almost Chinese: they would not stay long on whatever object she looked at. I had observed enough about women in the Copperbelt to know that eyes that refuse you are really seeking you out; those that open up for you have nothing to promise you.

Thus it was I said to myself, 'Chimba, here she is. Go get her.' I did. To me it was not even conquest. I always felt the drive to achieve something and simply took it for granted that I was going to own it. What people say — that you value something you have worked for — is true, but what you did not work hard for is not necessarily worthless. Monde took to me like that. I told her right from the beginning that I was married, had one child, that another was on the way, that I had lost the

43

firstborn.

'I have seen you come and go in the city,' Monde said. 'I have marked you as a man I would like to have. So your married life does not interest me. Not now. Because I couldn't do anything about it anyhow, could I? If you want to keep me and your wife, it is all right by me.'

'Would you rather take a man who can give you security as a legal husband?'

'It does not matter at present. When I want such a man, I will tell you. And if you don't want to be that man, you will tell me.'

What common sense! What a woman! I never stopped to brood over whether I should keep the one or the other — Tirenje or Monde. It was not important. I loved both very much. Each one fulfilled some part of me. And yet I could not bring myself to telling Tirenje about Monde, although I tried on the morning Tirenje talked about the python and the leopard. I felt I loved her more deeply when I had been to see Monde, who often came to the Copperbelt.

Again I felt rich, increased, to be loved by two women. Yes, that was it: to be loved by two women. More than that, I loved them both; each in a different way. To tell Tirenje would make me feel guilty of hurting her. Thinking back on it later, I remembered how the Hackett incident had rankled in me. So that I felt happier still that I could virtually say to the angels that were spying on me on his behalf: 'Tell him, go tell him that I'm free of his institutions!' But this was never in the forefront of my consciousness. It was only a soft voice, if even that, an awareness that Hackett never forgave me and that I needed no forgiveness anyhow.

The soft voice. I had to acknowledge at the same time, much as I hated to, a twinge of guilt. Not anything to deter me. Simply a soft voice that told me Tirenje would not like my relationship with Monde. Mornings as I lay in bed beside Monde, I would look up into the ceiling, thinking about Tirenje. Yes, there were nights when I did not enjoy Monde at all, because I dreaded the possibility that Tirenje might track me down to her lodgings. Sometimes I heard a voice outside in the yard which sounded like Tirenje, and my heart would kick me in the rib cage. Some days when I was in the big city, I would decide the very next day to drive back to Luanshya, longing to see Tirenje, to speak to her and the children, to hold her in my arms, to reassure her that I loved her. But always I would go to Monde with an aching hunger, a zest that seized me by the throat. I refused to contemplate giving up either one. I told myself, too, I was destined for great things. I just knew it . . .

I had seen more passionately demonstrative women than Tirenje. The woman who can pace the village or township, announcing publicly that she has caught another woman in bed with her husband; the one who can dig her nails into a rival and tear her clothes; the female who runs down the street crying and telling everybody that her husband has beaten her; the messy town female who wants to be seen with you in broad daylight for show-off. I say 'town' because in village life a woman would seldom do that. The injured wife will call the husband's relatives to discuss it. She will have received the teachings from the elders that you sit on family disagreements no matter how irksome, and solve them with your people. Came the preacher and gave us the idea from the pulpit that adultery must be publicly denounced, everything short of stoning the 'sinner'.

'How can I share my man with another woman!' Tirenje once said before we were married. 'Am I not enough to care for, feed, clothe, love and give you children? Look at us all here, we are all poor, we have to scratch for dirt to eat like chickens.'

'Suppose I earn enough to keep more than one?'

'I'm not an illiterate woman.'

'Why should an illiterate woman be able to handle one or two other wives of her man and you can't?'

'It is not a matter of *cannot*, it is that I would not have it.'

'Why? What is it that literacy has done that limits your capacity?'

'Because I know more.'

'Why?'

'Because I am literate. I selected you among many men. I have pegged my piece of land. No woman but me is going to graze in that land. When you know more — when you're literate, I think — I think — how can I say? — I think you become aware that there are certain things that should belong to you alone — a man, for instance.'

'Because you know more, because you are literate because you know more . . .'

We laughed the whole thing off.

Years later I puzzled over it. What is it in the printed word that, in expanding a woman's mental capacity, limits her capacity to tolerate others' claims on her husband's affections? If Monde had dramatized her demands in public I would have left her. She did not. Life was cosy for me that way.

Tirenje's words made me speculate a lot on the illiterate masses. The ACM often accused us of being an elite leadership. 'Do not listen to these educated men!' they told the people. 'They have learned the methods of the white man and they will trick you, they do not care about the sufferings of the common man.' Another wicked exaggeration of course. Many of the NAP leadership had only finished Grade Six or Seven of primary school. The most vocal in the whole party were mere fire-eaters or bleating goats. If ACM had merely said 'literate', it would have been accurate. But then that would also be a self-accusation. Where do the illiterate masses organize and lead themselves? They need leaders who can read the newspapers, the law, and interpret these to them ... What native capacity have we politicians lost in our education? I knew it had happened. I knew there was something lost, but as to what it was exactly I was stumped for an answer. I am sure that culture hyena, the Vice President of the NAP, never even asked himself this question. Mostly he tore into the bowels of the corpses of tradition ...

The present held me. Politics consumed much of my time. There was peace and love in my house. We called our daughter Wezi. She was born just before Independence. *Kwacha!* A new bright day had dawned. October 1964. I stood on the hill to see it come. Grandfather was so right. I felt big. Before that dawn, federation had scattered. It had become dead history, to be remembered only as a dream spanning 1953-1964.

The only thing that soured life a little for me and Tirenje was the news that my sister, Moyo's mother, had died, after a brief illness. Brief? I don't know. My people have been sick so long, oh so long. Forty-five seems a crucial age for us. Droughts, poor soil, mine labour — just the day-to-day effort to live — have burned us up. Those children laughing and rope-skipping in the dust wouldn't know that death is stalking them everywhere they go ... With a husband like Moyo's father, my sister stood still less of a chance. And yet it was ironic that he should survive her. A man like him, who was already in the swamp down there. Had no grit and yet continued to live, as if tied to a millstone, drowning every day of his life. My sister and Moyo had come to the funeral of our firstborn. I felt her death deeply. I went to the funeral, which I had to finance all the way in the abject circumstances I found in the home. Father came, but he might just as well not have. His mind was not with us at all.

'I shall have to live in the capital city now,' I announced to Tirenje.

'I know you will want to prepare your office and the house before the children and I come to join you.'

Tirenje. She always seemed to read my mind, just like that! And to think how I had worried over how I would tell her this. Silly, I thought, when there had been bigger things I did not feel the need to be apprehensive about telling her.

'I will come and get you or send for you.'

I did not fetch the family, I did not send for them. I did visit them. Once a month. My new job held me down in the big city. I sent them enough money regularly. Tirenje insisted she wanted to come and join me. I kept asking her to put it off for a while until I should feel easier in my Cabinet post. 'Let us visit you for a weekend then,' she pleaded in her letters. I relented on that. This was six months after I had moved into the big city. Monde was living with me. She spent that weekend away with friends.

I do not know if it was simply *my* nervousness, which I found difficult to acknowledge, or if it was a fact: Tirenje seemed to be suspicious. She went from room to room, as if she were sniffing around for clues. I had no reason to worry on *that* score. And yet, damn it, I did. That weekend I came within a painful inch of telling Tirenje all about it. Twice I tried — or should I say nearly weakened? Afterwards I was glad I hadn't. Oh how glad! I had justified to myself what I was doing. I knew better than to think I could justify it to Tirenje.

'I could be of use to you if I came to join you,' she said on Sunday morning as she brought me breakfast. She took complete control, as if she knew the house, had lived in it as long as I had. Cleaned and cooked and tended Wezi the baby. The four-year-old boy played around in the spacious yard. It made me feel good, this efficiency. Which irritated me also somewhat. Because I did not want to acknowledge Tirenje's superiority over Monde in practical matters of housekeeping. Monde was good in her own way at acting hostess to my important guests. She was smooth and graceful. Not in a superficial way. Her four years in Britain training as a secretary were well accounted for. She made protocol feel like a thing rolling on ball bearings, conducted at the same time with grace, self-confidence. Yet I felt something was missing in Monde. Something unnameable. Maybe something that keeps a woman's feet on the ground, as Tirenje's were. Tirenje was all there. With time she could adjust to protocol in the house and in public, she could dress less plainly. She had the will to do that. So I decided that the two women fulfilled two sides of me. I was going to leave it at that. I was not going to brood over the fact I knew so well, oh so well, that Tirenje would not accept such an arrangement. Some day I would resolve it. Things had happened to me that made me believe I had a charmed life. I was not made to sink down under. I postponed the ultimate resolution, which depended on me — wholly so. I said to myself: let things go the way they must. I even speculated comfortingly that Tirenje might not like big city life. A proposition I knew had very short legs.

So when she pleaded with me at breakfast, I merely said, 'I will see. Give me a little more time.' She fixed her eyes on me and then dropped them. The signal was clear. She was not going to surrender on this one.

A number of things happened in 1966 that concerned me deeply although I was not involved. Moyo arrived in the city with his grandfather, old Mutiso. His father had died the previous year — a quiet exit. I was made Minister of Transport and Works. This followed shortly after the head of government had become head of state also as President of a new republic, and as part of a Cabinet reshuffle. You don't ask questions when a reshuffle is made. But I suspected, indeed was almost certain, that it was a move to shut me up. Transport and Works! I had seen the colonial whites who worked in the Public Works Department out there in Shimoni and Kapiri. They ambled in shorts, mindlessly it seemed, into taverns at midday, with ochre-coloured legs and arms, ridiculously hairy and thick and elemental. How could I ever imagine that come *Kwacha* I would become their boss! I felt insulted. Some idiot of a commentator suggested in *Capricorn* that I might have offended the President with my tough line as Minister of Internal Affairs. That I had become a risk to the tourist industry and foreign investments by making the entry of visitors difficult, by expelling some whites from the country. The idiot! Wait till I move in the Cabinet, I thought. You'll be out in the street, crawling on your belly for crumbs. Together with the editor!

The big case during my regime in Internal Affairs was that of Joyce Mackenzie. Let out a scream in the office of the Minister of Agriculture. Rushed to the police to report that she had been raped. By whom? The Minister himself. A senior member of the Cabinet, highly respected, too. The Cabinet sat and chewed over the accusation. I instructed the police to investigate. The Minister flatly denied it. The girl had no eye witnesses. It had been after knocking-off time. Medical evidence of rape was irrefutable. A few days later I received a call to join the President for a working lunch. One of those he held at State House to have an opportunity to talk to individual guests about specific, often intimate affairs. 'I want you to give Joyce Mackenzie five hundred pounds and order her to leave the country,' the President said, with a deep frown. 'It won't be an order, really, but she couldn't bear the alternative. If she stayed on here, she could not find work anywhere. I'd make sure of that. Impress this on her English mind. Tell her legal proceedings would lead her nowhere. She is smart enough to understand the workings of power. The English always are.'

It was done.

At the airport the peacock shouted to a journalist who had clapped his ear to a keyhole to catch whatever leaked out, and obviously planned to be at the airport on that day. 'I was raped by a Cabinet minister! I'm leaving in disgust.'

The cub reporter had a field day asking leading questions in his paper. Some of which questions cast a shadow over my Ministry. No one, not the President, ever told the Cabinet if the Minister of Agriculture considered himself guilty at all.

I did not need to apologize. for my actions regarding immigration processes. The Minister of Health kept pestering me and my immigration officers about doctors who were waiting in Britain, India, Canada for their visas and work permits. He all but accused me of slowing down or frustrating recruitment from abroad. Some of these semi-literate ministers! Again the press picked it up. I had to put my foot down and get the President to caution the fatheads in his team. 'Some of my comrades,' I dared to say in a Cabinet meeting, 'need to go to school to learn procedure and the code by which a decent Cabinet should operate.' The President snorted, his Vice stared at me like an owl.

Then there was the case of the dozen refugees. I had them put in jail, not as criminals, but to await a new immigration law. What that law was going to be, I could not tell. The President simply said we needed to make a law. The Attorney General was going to get round to it some day . . . No African state has laws conferring immigration status on a non-native. You enter a country to study or to work or visit, on a permit. You apply for renewal and you get it or you don't. But the President instructed me to put these men in jail rather than hand them back to the regimes they had escaped from, or give them asylum ourselves. Any time they wanted to proceed to another country that would allow them to enter without the proper papers, they were free to go. We had refugees who were looked after by their freedom organizations. The President had even appointed a special government agent — Commissioner for External Liberation Movements — and we gave them a house whose offices they could share. The commissioner was crazy no doubt, one of the many blustering political clowns, but he was aware there was a job to do. If you asked him what it was exactly, he couldn't tell you. He was directly answerable to the President himself, and did not have to report to the Cabinet. The two newspapers we had made fun of him and he was flattered by it! Anyhow we could not waste able personnel on a post that was merely supervisory. The dozen refugees belonged to none of the organizations represented in our country. None claimed them. They might be spies acting for Portugal, Zimbabwe or South Africa. It was unthinkable that any one would remain unaffiliated in those countries, each of which had more than one freedom organization.

Capricorn made me look like a Nazi. All the eighteen months they had tried to revive the case of the dozen — the 'dead-end dozen,' as the heading went. The paper was certainly out to win applause as a champion of the refugees by distributing free copies, pushing them into the hands of diplomatic missions. The purpose was to try to influence these missions to ask their countries to adopt the refugees who wanted to leave.

Soon I was referred to in captions as 'the controversial Minister'. Sweden, Denmark, Yugoslavia had between them adopted six.

My successor had no sooner taken over than two skunks let him have it, one after the other, at short intervals. A black doctor from Namibia whom we had given political asylum as a refugee two years before had to be expelled. He had no papers to leave the country and was to be imprisoned until a country should offer him asylum. He fled, tried to cross the north-eastern border. He was returned by the border police to the capital. My successor asked what I would do in his position.

'I'm pressured,' he said frantically. 'I'm being pressured, man. The Ministry's involved and now the President is on top of me. If I refuse to expel the man the whole thing will blow up in our faces. After the Joyce Mackenzie case how can we ever be trusted by the electorate again, eh? — Tell me, just tell me!'

'Why are you being pressured, comrade?'

'I tell you and then the story goes round I told you and then I'm fired —'

'Forget it. You shouldn't be asking me what I think you should do if you won't say what the circumstances are. Stay with your troubles. I'm going back to my tractors and macadamizers. Kwacha!'

'The incompetents!' I muttered to myself as I went to my car. 'Frightened little Grade Five men handling portfolios too big for them, and I Chimba Chirundu have to run a ministry where your job is like holding a power drill with asinine persistence while it bores into the ground. Confounded incompetents!'

What a year 1966 was! The other stink that was to hit my successor came about as a result of pressure from another source. The Minister of Education had been unhappy with his Afro-American wife. It was one of the pub jokes: what does a man want with a foreign wife when there are so many beautiful girls in our country? . . . If a man thinks he's too educated for the woman he loves he can educate her himself — send her to school . . . Afro-Americans are black, what's the trouble? . . . Black, yes, but they're Americans . . . I mean would they understand that a man needs a concubine, would they? What you mean, man? Our own educated girls don't stand for that neither . . . Bar talk like that. The Minister pressured my successor. To avoid having to stamp the deportation order on her passport, he asked the American Embassy to warn the lady so that she would leave the country before the order was officially issued.

The effect was the same. She told the press at the airport that she was being sent out. The press reporters badgered my successor until he told them the Minister's wife had been found to be a security risk in the country. 'She was undermining the authority of the government.' 'In what ways?' 'That's all I have to say, gentlemen.'

Bloody goddamned incompetents! Congenital failures! The pressure my successor felt in the previous case must have been powerful enough to have impelled the President himself to hand down an order for expulsion. But the government was not going to care two rows of rusty pins if the Minister of Education and his wife were going to live a cat-and-dog life. He could just as well have divorced her and let her continue to live in the country. I couldn't see the President intervening on behalf of the Minister. So my successor could have refused. But maybe he had been bribed! I admire people who can wield power to their personal advantage. But even the Education Minister's power and also my successor's, however derivative, filled me with awe. I felt fearful. It suggested something I would like to taste, but with caution, lest I gorge myself until I grew horns and spikes! I smelled something sinister, as when you expect a leopard to leap from a rock and kill more than it can eat . . .

I thought in a relatively dull ministry like Transport and Works I would have time to think more about things, to reflect more creatively about matters outside of my province. I had miscalculated.

He came to see me in my office. 'He says he is Moyo, your nephew, sir,' my secretary said when I told her I was too busy to see anyone. He had tried three times already. On each occasion I did not have a moment to spare. 'You've told me several times who he is,' I said. 'Let him in.'

He was always full of beans, Moyo. A little bundle of energy and determination, as I was to discover two years later, to my disgust and dismay. Laughing twinkling eyes. Each of three or four times that we met at his home I had sensed an irrepressible something in him. Something I admired then, at a distance, but was to dread later, when I was to deal with it.

'Greetings, asibweni!'

'Greetings, son of my sister.'

After exchanging pleasantries here and condolences there, he came straight to the point.

'I told asibweni in my letter I was coming I tried three times to come in your secretaries are badly brought up I tell them each time I am your nephew you and my mother sat on the same man's knee I was told people in the city have no manners but I did not think it was like this . . .!'

My laughter cut him off short. The way he carried on without pausing to take a breath, I would not have come in otherwise.

'You don't realize, *mupwa*, son of my sister, this is a government we are running. If your own grandfather, whether my father or Old Mutiso, if any of them came to see me, I would treat them like I treat everybody else. I must show no favours to relatives.'

Moyo's mouth remained open a little longer before he said, 'I need a job, asibweni.'

'I'll do what I can. I am going to give you a letter to introduce you to the workshop manager in the Loco yard. If he has a job he'll take you. Loco is the yard where all government vehicles are kept. The Information desk will direct you to the yard. You know what I advise you to do? Go to the school of driving in the meantime. Driving jobs pay better. Less strenuous too in any Ministry. Who knows, you may even become my personal chauffeur. Information will also direct you to the better of the two schools in town.'

I wrote the note and gave it to him.

Moyo was as sharp as I had made out in the beginning. He got a job in the workshop. Three months later he came to see me.

'Thank you, asibweni. I have got my driver's license and the manager has hired me as a driver.'

'Tell you what, you're going to drive me to your place. I must see

Old Mutiso. I'll give him a surprise. This evening directly after work. I'll bring the car back myself to save you a bus journey.'

His eyes sparkled with life and anticipation. As if he were ready to take on the world. For sheer zip and enthusiasm, a go-ahead spirit — if we had ten of him in the Cabinet instead of some of the fatheads and fat-bellied worms we did have, this country would have little to fear.

It was good to meet Old Mutiso again. His face, his physique, his handshake, left an image in my mind of a patch of ground that has been ploughed, harrowed, ploughed, and harrowed year after year. Only his laugh, the twinkle in his eyes that showed even in the dim paraffin lamp on the table — only these seemed to defy the rain that had begun to fall soon after we had arrived, and was relentlessly beating down.

I have contempt and revulsion for lack of will in a man or woman while they still have the physical strength and an unimpaired mind. Old age draws me to itself. You look at old age and you seem to be in the presence of an awful mystery. One that commands reverence and at the same time seems indifferent. Like a four-year-old child, an elderly man will ask questions he doesn't care to hear answers to. And yet you feel compelled to listen to him. He is an ancestor now. Time has poured into this life all it could ever invest. This man, this woman you see in front of you in their seventies, eighties, nineties, has earned that status. In Europe and America, I've been told, they would be tucked away in a home, out of the concourse of general humanity. Or they would be confined in a private room in the house. Moyo would be seen as having towed behind him a wreckage for the scrapyard. To us, he would be walking beside a god . . . Even though I did not agree with my father, despised him for having been emasculated, I knew soon he would be one of the ancestors, so that the discords of our life would not matter any more.

I was sure that we were in for another exchange when I had a third letter from my father asking me to come home. Tirenje and the children were staying with him. I was sure because I hadn't had time to visit them in Shimoni. Moyo drove me to Shimoni. I would make official visits to the transport depots in the area at the same time.

'Your wife and children have gone home to Musoro,' my father said in a subdued voice. 'They waited and waited and then Tirenje said, she said, father you live on the little money Chimba sends you and I do not want to eat up all your food. She said, I must take the children to my father's house. I will be able to help him with that garden. She told me you had stopped sending money for four months.'

I did not feel in the mood to reply. Indeed I had failed to send them money. I was busy buying land in the city on which to build a house of my own. I could not bear the thought of being a government tenant any longer. Who knew, I might be fired one day, a coup might break upon us. Who knew? Who knows even now? That demotion had shaken me. Just that time. I knew I was destined for great things. I came to see the demotion as an event that should draw out the best in me for the climb that lay ahead.

'You know best,' my father said, as if to reply to my silence. 'You know best how to run your family, it is not for me to judge you. But it is a sin in God's eyes to abandon your children while you live as a big man in the city. It is a sin.'

'I will go to Musoro,' I said abruptly as if by reflex.

His face told me there was a thought bothering him, but it was a great effort to verbalize it. Bang it came as a question that made my heart miss a beat.

'Chimba,' he said, running his large sinewy hand over his whole face which was working, as if to steady it. 'Chimba, do you have someone living with you in the big city? Someone who has taken Tirenje's place?'

It was obvious throughout this meeting that he was trying desperately hard to subdue his emotions. I decided I should maintain that key.

I chuckled and paused and chuckled. I felt I was making myself a fool with this kind of response.

'How could I?'

He snorted and spat into a trash bucket at his side and snorted. 'You are not answering my question.'

'I do not have to. Did Tirenje tell you this?'

'What difference would it make who told me? The matter lies with your conscience. You are not answerable to me but to God. But I realize my God is not yours. I do not know you any more, Chimba, God forgive me! Go and comfort that good woman. She is married to a man not a government. Do you hear me? She needs a man. Even if she were starving it would not matter as long as she had her man by her side, not a — not a —' He took a deep breath and expelled it in exasperation.

'What about my two mothers?' I retorted, not without a little malice.

'They found other husbands, and I have prayed all these years that they have a better life than I could give them. God in the heavens is my judge.'

Yes, they did remarry. He was right. I could not tell whether he was feeling pity for me, in which case he must have felt superior. The speculation caused a constriction in my throat.

What did my father mean by *What difference would it make who told me? — The matter lies with your conscience?* I asked myself this question over and over again as we drove to Musoro. There was a regular bus service between the capital and the Copperbelt; lots of people made the distance by car — two hundred miles or so. People talk. Could Tirenje . . .? I made up my mind to deny it if I were confronted with the question, not to broach the subject on my own initiative.

It was evening when we arrived at the little farming town of Musoro, near the eastern border. They had had rain, and the smell of cow manure and savanna grass came on strong. The cry of crickets and cicadas pierced the cool air.

The children saw the car approach the house and I heard them yell to their mother. I had not seen them for four months and they ran toward me as I approached. Tirenje's face beamed with joy and surprise. That gave me a lift; the apprehension that was knotting up inside me, mixed with indignation, was coming under control.

'Who is that? *Moyo!*' she shouted as he came up to greet her. 'Oh we are so happy to see you again, Chimba! Has he not grown since I last saw him! We are so glad the gods have cared for you during your long journey. Papa, go and catch two of those fat chickens and make them ready for the pot.'

We always called our eldest son Papa because he was named for Tirenje's father.

'The rains were late,' she said as we went into the mud house, 'but the chickens are still thriving.' She looked thinner, but still carried herself well.

Her father came in from the garden. He was almost the living antithesis of my father. Shorter, slightly built, almost self-effacing. He had a lively face where my father's was grim. The ten years' difference between their ages was evident (he was 70). He was more approachable without evoking pity, like my father after he had got religion. Tirenje's father's Christianity was not loud-mouthed: he did not allow it to be a ruling passion. He was cynical about it at times, without acting so. He had hauled the fat Baptist preacher over the coals for writing the letter that precipitated the Hackett incident. Told him, as Tirenje reported with great amusement, 'No more chicken and fried eggs and tea in my

55

house, you hear me preacher man! No more! You hear me too, Tirenje, no more I say. You go pushing your belly from house to house peddling lies, spreading them all over like seed, badmouthing people who have done you or God no harm at all — in broad daylight when other men have gone to do an honest day's work. Why did you have to write to the white man? Is he your god also? Can you not ask your own ancestors to find out for you what the Almighty God wants you to do? Are you so muddle-headed you have lost your way to the ancestors? I am ashamed to be in your pants. The ancestors would have reminded you of the teachings of our elders — that a child is a human being whether he is born before or after marriage. Children are born and there is no sane law that will tell people when their children should be born. Even if Chimba does not in the end make my daughter a wife, the child is ours to cherish.' If I needed any moral support for what I had said to Hackett, this incident served me well. Tirenje's father had told the preacher not to visit his house again until he, the older man, would have asked his ancestors what to do about the preacher. 'No more,' he stressed.

Needless to say, the old man could not survive impeachment in the church council of elders. The American superintendent ordered his expulsion from the council. He told them they were free to do that but they were not going to drive him out of the church. They tried to do that but relented. From then onwards he sat with the other elderly men and women on the floor right at the back. As is customary in country churches where benches are few, the older people, like the children, sit on the floor, but at the back. They are thus saved the trouble of standing to sing or kneeling for prayer.

My father-in-law's helpers who lived nearby filled up drums with water and made open fires to heat it for our baths. It was a memorable night. Four months is nothing in a politician's life. But somehow as I went into Tirenje that night, it seemed like a long long time since my last visit at Luanshya. She was warm, responsive, receptive as ever, but it felt as if she was giving more than ever before. A few tremulous seconds I felt as if it might be the last. The very last . . .

'Tonight,' she whispered as we played around, 'hold me like a python, like in the old days.'

'A python does not spare the lungs of its victim.'

'I am a victim. Rather crush me than leave me again.' Indeed my arms seemed to take in the whole frame of her body.

In the morning Tirenje woke me up with breakfast.

'Moyo is up already,' she said, 'he is out in the field.' After she removed the tray and things, she came to sit on the bed, facing the wall.

'You are leaving me,' Tirenje said, looking alternately at the fingers she was wringing and at the wall. 'I have not told my father what is wrong.'

'I am not leaving you, Tirenje,' I said, 'what makes you think that?'

'I know it somehow, Chimba. I could feel you last night, I knew then that you are going to leave me. You are leaving me.' I knew she was crying softly. I sat up. I halfway stretched my arm to touch her shoulder. Then I could not, or would not. She turned round to face me, wiping her eyes with her gown.

'Take me with you then.'

'Let me go back to the city, and I swear I'll send a car to fetch you.'

'Chimba, you have said that so many times for three years now, and I cannot take it anymore. Take us with you now.'

Silence. Then again, 'You are leaving me, Chimba, you are leaving me.' She was crying aloud now.

'Not now, Tirenje, hear me, I will send for you, I swear I will.'

She looked at her hands. Then she stiffened. 'I have heard that you are living with someone. I do not want to believe it. But hear me, Chimba, please hear me, I will not mind living in the city, as long as you let me and my children live in a separate house.'

I was stunned. I couldn't be hearing that from her own lips!

'You do not believe that I will not make trouble for you. But hear me my husband, I will not. Let us come. These children need a father, a real father, not a guardian. I need a man to live with, not a caretaker. After last night I may carry a baby in me. I need to be where you are. Hear me my husband.'

I told her I believed her. Impulsively I said, 'You have heard right. I have a woman living in the house. You must have known that I could not be content with one wife.'

'Have you married her?'

'How can I when I am also married to you?'

'By customary law?'

'No.'

'Will you take us?'

'Yes. Pack your things and let us go.' I cannot remember how I came to say that, or even what my voice sounded like. Looking back on it now I think it was her mention of the children. The last three years when I agonized about the separation it was more the image of the children that gave me a sense of loss. I had full confidence that Tirenje had immense resources inside her. Only later did it occur to me how impulsive my answer was at the time. Her tears did not make things easier. Her words *you are leaving me* cut through me because they found me out, they infuriated me because they demanded of me a decision which I had postponed for three years. Postponed until it felt as if I had decided not to make a positive move. Throughout the three years something kept telling me if Tirenje loved me and cared passionately enough, she would fight for her rights. I mean she would want to find out what was going on in my private life in the capital city. And when she found Monde she would rave and want to tear her apart in order to establish her claim. By the same token I would also ascertain if Monde's love for me could absorb a confrontation and thereby prove to me its weight — both in tears and resilience. And every time I thought like this I was reminded that Tirenje was not demonstrative in those terms. But why, I asked myself, should she take me so much for granted? Doesn't she know a husband has to be fought for just as much as a woman has to be fought for? Men have killed for women . . . I had proven my love for both by keeping both . . . The debate would become more and more futile and unimportant. Futile, partly because a man has a special kind of relationship with a woman who has borne him children, which is itself the supreme demonstration.

I took the children out to the stream. For the first time that morning I felt what it would be like to be separated from them forever or indefinitely. I wanted to hold them to me with bands of iron. It is possible, I said to myself. It is possible. If this thing did not work out, I'd still want to keep the children. All the more reason why time and again to myself I rejected the idea of divorce.

Back in the capital, Moyo asked Ankhazi, as he called his aunt Tirenje in Tumbuka, and the children to come and stay with him in Kolomo Camp, while I sorted things out for better accommodation. Old Mutiso and Moyo slept in the front 'room' and Tirenje and the children in the only other one, with a crude cloth partition between them. I would have preferred to put them in a hotel but Tirenje would have none of it. Goodhumouredly she said, 'I have never been in a hotel in all my life and I would not know how to conduct myself.' She had been all excitement on the road, as if she was not travelling into the unknown.

I visited them every evening. I found them an apartment on the edge of the town and insisted they move out of Moyo's as they were too cramped. She relented.

Moyo came to tell me about it. 'Asibweni, I am sorry very sorry about what happened. I should have asked you before. I was stupid. Asibweni!'

'Will you make some sense?'

'Mai wamung'ono asked me not to tell you.'

'Tell me what?'

'She asked me to take her to your house during the day. So I took her there during my lunch break. It is so near. We found Miss Lundia. I introduced them. Oh I am so foolish, asibweni.' When Moyo did not use the Tumbuka *ankhazi* for aunt, he called Tirenje *mai wamung'ono* in Chinyanja. He called me *asibweni* — uncle in Chinyanja. It irritated me that he never addressed Monde as aunt or even sister. I regarded this as a value judgment, which said a lot about his idea of himself.

'Get to the point, Moyo, I've no time to be wasting here!' Anger pushed up my gullet.

'Yes, I'm sorry, asibweni, sorry! They quarrelled. Bitterly. I don't know who started exactly but it must have been mai wamung'ono because, I do not know why, Miss Lundia could easily have started it. The gardener had to come in because they were going to rough each other up any moment.'

I postponed talking to both Monde and Tirenje about the incident beyond the preliminary 'I hear there was trouble here during the day . . . What happened? . . . Sorry to hear that . . .' Both were uncommunicative anyway that evening, and the next day I was going out to a dam site two hundred odd miles south to examine transport plans for workers who would be engaged in the project. In the morning as we drove down, I told Moyo that he shouldn't worry about the incident anymore. I was glad it had happened in my absence. I had not consciously created the setting for it either. And it wasn't as if I had paid to watch a cockfight. Something was bound to give.

Tirenje and the children were gone when I returned the following day. A letter awaited me at the apartment. The furniture was intact, the interior quite orderly. It was the kind of letter people write who forget most of what they learned about punctuation. Or, when they write in their native tongue, they find punctuation tedious, a nuisance in the flow of their thoughts. Tirenje always wrote to me in Chinyanja:

Beloved husband,

We have gone back to my father. I went to your house a house I would have been happy even thankful to call my own. I would have been happy Chimba I wanted to see with both eyes I saw with my own eyes I did not quarrel with your girlfriend she tells me with her own mouth that you are not married by law your girlfriend is not the fighting woman what pierces my heart like a spear is when she says to me she says when are you returning home? I ask which home? She says Musoro. I stand up on my two legs I shout to her I say are you married to my husband by law? She says no I say by the white man's law? She says no I ask again I say by the law of the Bemba? She says it is not my place to ask such questions I tell her Chimba is my husband did he not tell you that? She says you told her why are you keeping him? I ask she says Chimba is keeping me I say we were not born yesterday you know my meaning I am not here to play house like you I want my man give me back my man she says I should tell you that Chimba I should tell you that I want you back she says tell Chimba that and hear his own words. Chimba knows I love him you tell him and hear the words from his own lips. I know my man my own man I asked her questions as if I had not said to you that I would live in the city as your wife even if you had another woman. I got angry I shouted like a mad woman I wanted to tear my clothes off my body and tell her how cheap she was but the man working outside comes in and asks us not to fight I say to him I say I am not going to soil my hands with dirt like her does she think because she is a city woman she is clever and I am stupid? She rushes me but the man keeps her away these are my words husband. Do not say bad words to Moyo he does not know what to do when older people quarrel and fight these are my words I swear by Mirimba's and Chirundu's ancestors they are true. When I was back with the children I say to myself I say Tirenje daughter of Mirimba go back to the house of your father there is no life here. I was wrong to think that I could do it Chimba I was wrong you know your own heart you must do what you think I have this to say from my heart I asked you at Musoro I said do you have another woman? Deep inside my heart I told you a lie to say that I could live in the city even if you have another woman deep inside my heart I wanted to hear from your own mouth hear you say you have another woman what I have heard friends and enemies tell me in Luanshya you said it but I still hoped my ancestors hear me truly Chimba I hoped that my heart would turn round and I would see things your way. It is not possible. Tell me what to do tell me what to do I

*will listen. For three years now we have not talked Chimba my husband
let us talk even by letter but come to Musoro let us talk that is what
people must do they must talk with their elders with parents uncles
aunts friends and heart and mind will settle down. Tell me what to do
tell me what to do.*

I am your wife Tirenje.

Why did she have to spoil the whole thing! I muttered to myself in
the centre of the apartment lounge. Why? Foolish woman! How foolish
women can be! When they are not trampled underfoot they put up
stupid meaningless fights! So you drew the confession out of me by a
trick! You couldn't even wait to see if the thing would work . . . if I
had taken you to the house there wouldn't have been this stupid quarrel . . . But you couldn't wait to muck it all up, no, not you . . . You
knew all along you didn't have it in you to make it work and yet you
let me go to all this trouble and then almost precipitated a scandal. As
if I didn't have enough enemies in my line of work! I've tried, you
know I did try and you mucked it up . . .

'That South African, asibweni, is a very good teacher. Not in all my
school life have I had such a teacher.'

'Who? You mean er — er —'

'Mr Letanka,' Moyo said. 'Mr Studs Letanka.'

'Oh yes, I forgot you go to that College of Public Education in the
evenings.'

'This man is just wonderful.'

'What does he teach you?'

'General History. We are now studying the trade union movement.'

'Why are you suddenly taken up with the trade union movement?
History I can understand, but this other thing.'

'I am a worker, asibweni, I have a natural interest in the organization of labour.'

'What does he teach you in the second subject? Strikes?'

'That and several other things.'

'Does he try to incite his classes?'

'How can he do that when he's working for an international organization?'

'Yes, yes, I know, don't try to be smart with me. They operate under cover of these international agencies often.'

'Do you think these United Nations agencies we have harbour people who hate us, asibweni?'

I knew I had started something which would create doubt in Moyo's mind. That was good.

'You don't mean you've been hobnobbing with people in such high places, my country nephew?'

He was silent for a few seconds.

'I've not been anywhere near there. But you frighten me.'

A moment of silence again. Then: 'Asibweni, Studs Letanka is a black South African. How can he be our enemy?'

'Why do you think I put the first lot behind bars? Look nephew, hear me: you are still new in the city. You are still only 21. You don't know much at all about these things. We're a new nation and we have got to forget all these fancy ideas about strikes and help the government. The people elected us. We know best how to run the country, that is why the majority elected us.'

'You do not believe in strikes, asibweni?'

'In colonial times, yes. Under African rule — no, strikes are not the right method at the moment. It's too early for that. They would paralyze the country when we're just recovering from colonial rape.'

'But asibweni, the copper mines are owned by foreign companies, white people, there are many South African whites working as miners, are these not dangerous people? They come and go back to their country for their holidays.'

'Their time will come, just you wait. But we're not going to be able to drive them out if our workers make trouble with the government. You know a family that is divided cannot cope with hostile forces from outside, is that not so?'

'Yes I agree, asibweni. But to organize trade unions is not mainly to start a strike, is it?'

'Just be careful what you let yourself in for.'

Yes, Moyo was too smart for his age. At twenty-one I was finishing teacher training, and my eyes were also beginning to open. But I was in school, whereas Moyo had gone to work after junior secondary school. What business had he to presume to learn about such complex things as trade union organization? In an institution for further education he should have been busy continuing conventional schooling — high school for instance, or a vocational trade. He needed that discipline. It didn't matter to me that most workers are illiterate and semi-literate, a thought that *did* occur to me. But damn it, this boy gave me the uneasy feeling that he wanted to be in the forefront. That's what annoyed me. As for that South African Studs Letanka — these smart South Africans — I've had them up to my eyes and ears. Even when they are refugees they behave like people who think the rest of Africa owes them something. They talk back, like to argue, strut about with round-shouldered arrogance — the teachers think they know a lot about the right philosophy of education for Africa, the nurses feel so sure of themselves in the hospitals. We must send more people overseas to study: we need our own personnel. Studs Letanka indeed! Must we, when we want aid, have exiles like him who come riding on the back of international money, after being picked up in the metropolitan centres of Europe?

Several times I felt the urge to visit the family. I kept putting it off, telling myself that duties were pressing. In reality I could have snatched a weekend for the four-hour car trip. Whenever I was about to decide, it seemed heavy iron chains were clapped on my feet. I could not move. I continued to excuse my immobility until it seemed rational for me not to move. I resorted to writing short letters at short intervals to Tirenje. She wrote to say she was pregnant. Another letter followed, dated 15 March 1968.

My husband,

I write this in bed after breaking the calabash I carried from the river as our elders say I had hoped for a girl I would have loved it and the seven months now seem such utter waste Turn those months into seven years and it seems that is what our married life has been a miscarriage you will know if it only appears so why have you left me Chimba why? What have I done wrong? I have mothered your children I have been a good wife to you why Chimba? I keep asking why does a man want to hurt the woman he loves? Why when you knew that I could not live with a second wife did you go ahead and take her? Was it because you despise me it is equally difficult to think otherwise First you know what I think and you go ahead and take another woman If you knew you were one day going to take a new wife why did you marry me and after marrying me why did you not divorce me? I would not have stood in your way I would not want to tie a man to my bed if he wanted to be free of me and it horrifies me to think that you might have known when you married me that you were going to keep me as a wife for your country pleasure and keep a wife for your city pleasures one who knows how to smile for people in high places one who knows how to walk like white people one who takes out a handkerchief for everything

that comes out of her face tears mucous saliva so as not to remove the
paint If you wanted to keep me as a wife you love why did you do
something you knew would hurt me would tear me apart? You are free
to divorce me Chimba you should have felt free to do so long ago but at
thirty-one I am prepared to go back to the Copperbelt with the children
where I will find work to bring them up I do not want your money if
you want to buy them anything or save it for them that is your own
business for me you should not worry It is finished.

 Your wife Tirenje.

Tirenje, Tirenje, you do not understand, I thought. You will never understand. The forces tugging at me from all sides — how can I understand them myself? That letter felt like a heavy lump of rock in my hands. I found myself trembling at the fingers. Her words pierced like sharp needles.

 I travelled to Musoro. I begged Tirenje to defer her decision to go to the Copperbelt; that she come to the city where she could get good medical care. She countered that there was a good gynaecologist in the Copperbelt. Which was true. A black South African again, damn it! I told her to wait for word from me about the matter of divorce. I told her it was not going to be an easy decision to make because I still loved her. She looked pale and worn out. I left full of fear and doubt. Something told me her mind was settled.

 Divorce would have been the easiest thing. But I did not want to lose her and the children. Not Monde either. Monde had become a habit I could not shake off; a convenient habit. Tirenje was a kind of home, the shelter a man comes back to after wandering from the cattle post; part of the reason for being alive, as basic as food and clothing. More than just a habit, without implying that Monde is one of these instant indulgences. Previously I had thought I could make Tirenje understand this: that she was this kind of shelter, that my love for her would not diminish. Married women know this all the time, perhaps, but — how do I know? — Women of Tirenje's generation invest all they have in one man and see no reason why the man cannot be like them.

 Some members of the Cabinet began to talk louder. People in taverns were also whispering and amusing themselves. Monde was feeling the heat. The President told me I would have to decide to divorce or chuck Monde. In sheer defiance and anger I took Monde to the marriage officer on 23 May 1968. Fortunately his fat nose had not got the smell yet, the whispers had passed his small rat-like ears by. He made me swear to my statement that I had married by Bemba traditional law, and that my marriage to Monde therefore annulled that first one. I told Monde to say I had dissolved the first marriage if ever she had to give an account of herself. She needed that protection. What she did not then know was that I had, after my marriage to Tirenje by traditional law, registered it under the colonial Ordinance.

I was playing for time. I thought, as I could not convince Tirenje that I was not being malicious, that I had the best intentions in the world, that a two-wives situation was worth trying. I would need to create circumstances that would show her the necessity to stay with me. How I was going to do that I did not know. I needed time to plan. With official heat diverted from my ass, my mind might function better . . .

It did not. Tirenje must have contacted a lawyer to investigate me. Or somebody put her up to it. Yes, somebody did it — Moyo, Che Chimimba the Prosecutor, some baboon-sucking malicious creature who's after my blood . . . As the number of possibilities and probabilities milled in my head I stomped and chafed in my office and forbade anyone to come and see me or telephone. Later it dawned on me that Tirenje was quite capable of initiating the process herself. Quite adequate to it . . . I felt a chill in my bowels . . .

I could not have made a worse move at this time — three weeks before I received the summons. I decided to move against government drivers. There were several who kept official vehicles out beyond 5 p.m. without permission, for their own private use. I knew some of them were ordered by Cabinet ministers and Permanent Secretaries to drive them out to their concubines, to bars, to night clubs, cinemas. My aim was to shake the earth under their asses in retaliation, to discredit them.

I drove around these places, except the houses of the concubines, which I could not locate. I netted fifty vehicles in a week. Sacked the drivers. That was when some came to me and reported which Minister ordered which driver to take them to what places. All the same I sacked some and suspended others. The officials were reprimanded by the President. I was elated. But the drivers were bitter. The executive committee of the Transport Workers Union, newly registered, came to see me to talk. Moyo was among them as secretary. They wanted their fellows to be given back their jobs and the ministers disciplined. I was adamant. I told them the racket had stopped, after this no driver need fear victimization. The committee left and gave notice of a strike which they were going to use to force me to bring back the workers.

I was determined to make myself heard in the Cabinet. I was going to take advantage of a meeting to be held at the weekend. I knew the members would say I was trying to drag into the river with me people I did not like as the last act of a sinking man. No matter, I thought. Let them think what they please, I must be heard anyhow.

'Mr President our leader and comrades,' I began. 'We know that one of us was guilty of molesting Joyce Mackenzie, but we hushed up the affair in a way you all remember. We also know that one of us wanted the Namibian doctor out of the way because he refused to perform an abortion on a female friend of a Minister. People will run around in panic when such things happen, as if a so-called illegitimate child is not a human being and must be destroyed; as if a wife were such a terrible unforgiving judge that she would set up a torture machine, as if the grandparents of a so-called illegitimate child would disown it and like Europeans send it to an institution. We also know why the minister of Education leaned on my successor the Minister of Internal Affairs to deport his American wife. In each of these cases, Mr President, the people concerned overreacted, out of panic; took steps that were out of proportion to the thing that confronted them. Are we going to use political power to solve our own domestic problems? If so, what is going to happen to government? Are we also going to use government as a cover for graft, bribery, brothel practices, as in so many countries of the western world where so much crime is institutionalized? I have said my piece, Mr President, thank you.'

'I'm sure Comrade Chirundu is exaggerating the gravity of the situation,' the President said after taking a deep breath. There were sighs of relief when he said this. Even timid smiles. 'The government is the first since independence and we are not about to allow laxity, graft, bribery and so on and so forth. No, no! I'm sure our comrade is overwrought. Tomorrow morning after a good night's rest he will feel better and he will see things in clearer perspective.'

The President made a few empty jokes to help the atmosphere to thaw. More timid laughter among the comrades. Idiots! Baboon-suckers! But for the admiration and respect I had for the President I'd tell you all what stuff some of you are made of, what stuff you've eaten. Cowards, sycophants who wear out their bellies crawling today and tomorrow, run around like headless chickens, political clowns, culture mongers who can't see further than the tip of their status walking-stick . . . And then you laugh. Some skunk is going to breathe into your mouths while they're open. One day you'll laugh yourself out of government road down the precipice. Pity that you'll drag us all down with you!

Although I felt relieved, I also felt exhausted. Unutterably weary in body and spirit. I wondered about my own situation in the whole pattern of power manipulation. Was I myself untainted? Did I look at Tirenje and Monde from a position of power? I was not sure, I was not sure, how does one know about these things when you have not planned them from the beginning, when you are obeying the orders of a passion too fiery, too powerful for you to even try to analyze?

When the summons came I thought I might use the trial as a platform to speak up against the ridiculous situation colonial marriage law had placed us in, an essentially polygamous people. Then I realized the hopelessness of such a crusade. Too many people preferred concubines in private and respectable marital relations in public. So I told my advocate, Mr Clare, to put on an act. I was suddenly overwhelmed by an irrational but crushing boredom about the trial . . .

'Things have not changed between us, understand, Monde? — Not a bit.'

'I understand, Chimba.'

'I'll come back — this is just a brief setback, but I'll return. You'll wait for me — but don't stay in that house alone during the strike. Get the police to guard it — or perhaps you could call your brother to come and live with you, but get the police all the same —'

'Yes, I'd better call him here, I can arrange for him to take night classes at the College — I'll wait, Chimba, I told you before, I can wait.'

'I know you will.'

'I'll bring you the papers and books you want.'

'Only the books — no newspapers — not for a week. Collect them and bring them all at the same time after a week. Only the books.'

'Stay in peace, dear.'

When she has gone, I wonder why I did not ask if *she* thought things had changed between us, after that little squall. But perhaps my instinct tells me we're still spitting out grains of sand and rubbing our eyes. If things have changed or are changing, time enough to know . . .

Yes, I've plenty of time to think. Close on ten years now since I got into politics. So much has telescoped in that span of time there has been almost no time to reflect. I'll read and study too, collect my mind, try to understand — what? I'm not even sure. I'm boiling over with indignation just now — after that circus. And then I also feel numb somewhere inside me. Too numb to care about those things they call the lessons of independence — whatever these big-headed theorists mean ... Time enough to reflect on them ... For now, these ten years have confirmed me in my belief that I am destined for great things ...

Chieza: How are the bowels this morning, friend?

Pitso: They worked well early this morning.

Chieza: Well and good.

Pitso: I've made up my mind. When I'm released from here, rain or shine, bless that day, I'm going back home.

Chieza: Home where, man?

Pitso: South Africa of course. Think I've got amnesia?

Chieza: That's where you're going to get it, black boy! Dashet! what do you think you're going to do there?

Pitso: Live, man, live. Better alive in hell than rot in a freezer.

Chieza: It's straight to jail you're going.

Pitso: Right. I go to the border and say I've come home. They say Pitso Mokae, wanted for trial under the Suppression of Communism Act and for leaving the country without proper papers, blah, blah, blah. Maybe even for terrorism. What'll they give me? Maybe three years. They can't prove terrorism. I've spent two years and fifteen months in this hole. At least when I get out there I'll be alive among my own people. I've asked you this before comrade — have you ever longed for your people so badly it seems to drain your blood? Leaves a dull ache here in the chest. Like you're standing on the bank of a river that can't be crossed and they're standing on the other side beckoning you to come and they say *come, if you can't, stay there 'cause we are not going to leave our homes.* Hell, man, it gives you an ache in your bowels you can't get used to or don't want to get used to. It's like something inside's going to bust and then there's no way except backtrack and they might put you together again back there.

Chieza: Mm, maybe, chum. Me, I want to collect myself and store energy and I don't want to burn up inside banging on steel gates before we are ready to move together without fear for our skins.

Pitso: I'll soon be forty. I reckon by the time I finish my sentence down there I'll be 45. But it'll still be progress, man, progress, moving *some*where, man.

Chieza: Suppose, just suppose, son of Africa, suppose any of these organisations in exile didn't also suspect us of being spies. Simply because they were already banned, eh? I mean banned when *we* became active wherever we were, came out without any movement to cover us — suppose they said they could have us?

Pitso: I could have joined them, twenty-four or eighteen months ago. I'm still a nationalist, but I think it's the people down there who'll decide when they've had enough of tyranny. Before *they* move, ain't no mother's son going to do fuckall outside here that will liberate anybody.

Chieza: I know, I wouldn't know how to decide. The tribalism and petty bureaucracy, useless diplomatic missions they maintain abroad, redundant talk talk talk they do in numerous worthless conventions, the faction politics — they make me want to scream. But I've always been a one to wait and wait and wait. You know, like a donkey can stand for hours in the rain and only now and again shake its ears or stamp on the ground. I wish I could join these fighting braves in Mozambique and Angola. Honestly, I often wish it. See how they're boring in, inch by inch.

Pitso: I've no use for that kind of patience, son of Africa.

Chieza: That beating up you got in detention. Have you forgotten that?

Pitso: Don't. No, don't touch that, don't remind me of it!

Chieza: If you can't forget you must remember. Maybe that memory will save you from this fool thing you want to do.

Pitso: How can I forget! The bellowing, oh that bellowing. I feel a shiver in my bones to think of it!

Chieza: Strapped by the legs from an iron beam with head facing down, right? The unmentionable things that they did to you — standing those seventy-two hours at a time in solitary, all those endless questions they took in relays — standing seventy-two hours while they grill you.

Pitso: Don't remind me of them, do you think I've not lain awake nights, every night in this jail — thought, remembered, heard my mate's screams. He'd refused to talk. Most of us lied but it was talking. When you don't talk the other man can't reach you, that makes him mad. So beating you up is a way of breaking you in, even if he knows you'll still be beyond his reach. He'll bust you open, even if all he gets is the blood and the gut and bellowing. Why do you remind me of this?

Chieza: They broke him, as I recall. They had to take him to a mental hospital?

Pitso: Don't. No, don't touch that, don't remind me of it. Bust him open, man, scorched his testicles with electric wires, all they got was a screaming and bellowing. Those chimps got nothing after all from us. We lied most of the time like a fake watch. Don't remind me — the mental hospital had him released, sent back home. All his wife was getting — remnants of a man once big and strong and vital. A mixed up head.

Chieza: And you're going back into *that?* Foolish black boy!

Pitso: Can't be worse than it is here. Don't remind me of it. Don't let me think of it! (*He weeps, turning his head away at intervals to avoid Chieza's eyes. As always at moments like these, his hands tremble. Moyo comes in.*) Hei there comrade!

Moyo: Hei friends!

Pitso: What do you think of the trial? Dull don't you think?

Moyo: Break-up of marriage has dramatic interest, talking about the causes and effects is a dull business. But they're my people. (*Pitso raises an arm to indicate the wish to close the subject.*)

Moyo: No, no. You misread me. There's so much to talk about. The transport strike. My uncle is hopping like a pumpkin pip in the fire. Says I've betrayed him as his nephew.

Chieza: Your aunt Tirenje — how's she bearing up to all this?

Moyo: Of course she made the first move. Damn right too. Took the stand this morning. Calm and dignified I tell you. But I could sense something dark and speechless beneath her calm. And yet she does not show any sense of triumph at all.

Pitso: Is she sure he'll be found guilty?

Moyo: Oh it's a foregone conclusion.

Chieza: Think it's being staged? I mean I can't imagine an educated man doing this kind of thing.

Moyo: Let's just say it was inevitable. He knew it would come to this one day I'm sure. Now take a look at the front page of this morning's paper. (*Chieza takes the paper.*) Two Angola Portuguese caught crossing the western border. The bastards! It's not enough they bomb our villages but their scum must spill into our country.

Pitso: The government will rough them up?

Moyo: Who knows anymore what the government will do these days? I just wish this Portuguese dung hadn't shown up just now. They could steal our thunder and the people may give us only divided attention. You should see and hear them today. All kinds of speculation — 'Shoot the pink Catholics!' they say. 'Shoot them in broad daylight!'

Chieza: What do you hear through the grapevine, Moyo? I mean from *high* places. (*Rubs his hands together in mock expectation.*)

Moyo: Nothing, except I hear say they're going to be tried immediately.

Pitso: Goddamn it! A snivelling zero-grade country, backward, illiterate like Portugal, shitting on this continent for four centuries!

Moyo: Oho, here comes your boyfriend. (*Warder approaches noisily.*) Can't wait for me to leave so he can enjoy your company.

Warder: Time up, time up! In the name of the President it's time up! Kwacha! (*He marches with a baton in the left armpit.*)

Moyo: (*Leaving*) If you don't see me in the next few days, know I'm tied up with the strike.

Chieza & Pitso: We thank you, son of the soil!

Chieza: Africa, Africa! The Europes are having a good time on this our continent, eh? They can rain urine on us any moment like chickens on a perch and they know we'll hold out our hands if we don't want the ground messed up, or else we'll clean it up. Tell me, son of Mokae, son of the soil, what is wrong with us Africans? I mean an African will kick you in the ass if a white man told him to do it. He shouts when he speaks to you like this *kwacha* clown but he trembles and stutters and scratches his head when he's face to face with a white man, like he was being blinded by the sun. Why so? I mean the white man knows this. He knows you're not going to fart in his presence. You're going to say 'Sichoos me please, sir, m'go out,' — you know, like we used to do as kids in class when you wanted to go out for a pee. Just to go out and blow a fart you've got to ask Europe's permission so you can stay clean in his presence. Kids are even more intelligent when it comes to that because they'll just let the class have the full benefit of a stink there on the spot.

Pitso: And yet you look at our ghetto toughies at home, son of Chieza. Those street boys have no respect for the white man. They call him 'little master' when they want something — like a bit of mercy from a ticket examiner on the train when they have no ticket or money, or from a cop when they want to insult him. They murder the Boer's language or tear it to shreds in sheer defiance. No, it's a certain breed of African, one who *thinks* he has much to lose if he acts uppity.

Chieza: Like with us in Zimbabwe. But look at the so-called independent man in Africa, educated or semi-literate or illiterate. What has he to lose by telling the white man to go fuck himself. Or how?

Pitso: Power, son of Africa, power. The white man spells power: machines, transport, communications, law, money, the word of a terrifying, finger-wagging god riding on fat books and fat aeroplanes moving on all kinds of wheels. Once he baptized us with his own urine, Europe's power was always going to fix us in a kind of stupor. Until — *(shrugs his shoulders)*.

Chieza: Until?

Pitso: Who knows? If we didn't hope for that day you and I wouldn't be here. I couldn't like Chirundu and his kind one bit, but I see them as men wielding power they don't understand. Plus they had a touch of Europe's pee on their foreheads once.

Chieza: Your *language,* son of Africa!

TIRENJE

April 3, morning

State Advocate Wanika stands up. The next witness is Tirenje Chirundu, née Mirimba, he announces.

Your name is Tirenje Chirundu?

Yes.

You want an interpreter?

Yes, I want to speak Chinyanja.

Is the accused in this case your husband?

Yes.

When did you get married?

November 1959.

Do you have children by him?

Yes. Two now.

What ages?

Eight and four.

Are they the only ones you ever had by the accused?

The firstborn died, the most recent one was a miscarriage — last year March.

Were you married by customary law or according to the Marriage Ordinance? You understand the difference between them?

Yes. We first registered under customary law and then under the Ordinance.

How far did you go in school?

As far as first year of junior high school. Finished Grade 7.

Did you teach after that?

Yes.

Have there been any proceedings for dissolution of this marriage between you and the accused that you know of?

No.

The marriage is still subsisting?

Yes.

You still regard the accused as your legally married husband?

Yes.

I have no further questions, my lord.

Any questions, Mr Clare? the judge asks.

Yes, my lord. Is it not true that you were married according to Bemba Law and Custom?

We did that in the first place, then we registered the marriage under the Ordinance.

Did you ask the accused why he decided on the second step?

I wanted a marriage that did not allow for more than one wife.

Did you respect his wish to marry according to customary law?

Yes. I said I did not mind as long as we did the second thing.

Did he ever express the desire to have more than one wife?

Only vaguely so. But he said he was happy to do as I wished. He loved me.

The accused is going to say that he was under the impression that the marriage under customary law would always be in force, no matter whether you turned to the Ordinance or not. Would you agree?

I do not know about what he thought, but I do know the officer who read the Ordinance to us warned us that he could not marry us if either of us was still married to someone else under the Ordinance. Also that if either of us was married by customary law, that union was dead from then onwards.

The accused will say that you left him in the capital. Your father did not bring you back or write to him to inquire, which is what happens in Bemba law, and he therefore considered the first marriage by Bemba law was dead, the only marriage he recognized. What will you say to this?

How can you marry by the Ordinance and decide that you do not recognize it?

Mrs Chirundu, I am here to ask the questions, not you.

Then I have nothing to say about a man who chooses which law to recognize and which to ignore.

I have no further questions for this witness, my lord.

Next witness: Wilson Mulemba. The officer who married Chimba

Chirundu and Tirenje Mirimba on 3 November 1959 in Kapiri. He produces two certificates, one indicating Bemba customary law, the other the Marriage Ordinance. He warned the couple, he confirms, on the matter concerning previous marriages. Did the accused sign the affidavit according to the Ordinance by which he swore that he had not previously márried by the Ordinance? Yes.

I have no further questions, my lord.

Are you sure that the accused signed the affidavit?

You were shown the document, Mr Clare.

Do you remember the couple?

Vaguely.

Nine years is a long time, isn't it?

I don't have to remember the faces of people who come to me, that's why we have signatures.

You are here to answer specific questions, Mr Mulemba, not to teach me procedure! I have no further questions for this witness, my lord.

Will the witness step down? Thank you, Mr Mulemba.

State Advocate Wanika confers with the judge.

This court will adjourn until tomorrow morning at 9 o'clock. Permission is granted for the accused to attend a Cabinet meeting. I want you to impress on the mind of the accused that come what may he has to be here tomorrow morning.

As Chimba rises to go out, Tirenje calls aloud to the State Advocate. By the time he has reached her seat she shouts, 'I want to speak!' The court stirs. The people stand still. 'I must speak!' she shouts again. She waves the bulky advocate aside and moves to the centre of the floor, facing the judge. 'I want to say all that is in my heart. You see this heart of mine? It is full of things, bitter things. I am going to speak and all the world must listen. I have been waiting for this day to come. Hear me all of you! I say hear me!'

State Advocate apologizes to the judge on her behalf. 'I have done nothing wrong, nothing!' she wails. Advocate holds her gently but firmly and leads her away and out through the side door, saying repeatedly, 'Calm yourself, you have answered the questions well, it is enough, the judge has heard, you are not being accused here at all, be calm.' 'I want to tell him,' she was saying, 'I want to tell him more — everything that has happened, the pain that lies here in the breast of a woman — I am not a woman of the street you hear me?' 'Yes, I know, I —' 'You must know — that man in there married me out of love and my father let me out of his house in proper decent manner —' 'Yes I know, I know, please sit here while I go into the court.'

Chimba, like everybody else, has been standing in his position, as if glued to the floor. The last words he hears her say as she is led through the door are 'Why will they not listen to what I want to say?'

'Mai wamung'ono,' Moyo says, 'all of tonight again our committee will be working. The good woman here, your msuweni, will let you stay with her until this whole thing is over. You will be comforted. I will see you at lunchtime tomorrow.'

April 3, evening

'You can talk to me, Tirenje, and cry as much as you want. It will be good. Talk to me while I knit.'

'You have known Chimba a long time, I believe. Once he talked about you when he returned from the city — my msuweni, he said, wants to meet you. Yes Cousin, we grow away from our families. But when a man goes into government, his wife and children are losing him to the people. Your mothers sucked from the same breast, and yet you saw very little of him even when he came to living in the big city. I am a newcomer in your family. I feel lost. I need strength. You lost your own husband, but the ancestors took him. You look so strong, msuweni, give me some of it, I seem to be losing my mind.

'Why did they refuse me to speak this morning? What is the reason? What do they know about the thirteen years I and Chimba have been together? They do not know the good years when we were happy. Since 1954, did he tell you? When I had his child in my belly in 1958 I did not care what church people said. I was happy to carry Chimba's seed in me. And then his government job, his life in the big city. They know nothing about these last four years — did the government have to take you away from me Chimba? When our people began to rule this country was the woman to lose her man, children their father? It does not matter any more Chimba son of Chirundu. Why am I asking these questions? We could have grown up together, and this is what we have come to — quarrels in court in front of strange people when we could have spoken to our uncles aunts cousins brothers.

'I can see you sitting there waiting to tell the people why you went and married another woman — what will you tell them Chimba? Did you have to pay so much for your government work? I did not want another wife in our house and yet you went ahead and took her — why, Chimba? Msuweni, did Chimba tell you we were unhappy together? No — he could not unless he wanted to tell a lie.

'Moyo tells me, msuweni, that Chimba could not understand why I should move against him like this — report him like a criminal — instead of allowing him to divorce. But you know, Chimba, you are a man of the government — they would come after you even if I had not set the dogs after you — you must have known what you were doing. Msuweni I also hoped that the court case would bring Chimba down from that high building in government and he would then see us down below more closely, know us again. Now I see that I could only take you back if your heart told you to come back.

'I had to find out about your city woman one day Chimba. People talk, they like stories about men in high places — you knew all this — why then did you continue to hurt me? Msuweni I have known that Chimba was the kind of man who would have liked two faithful wives, like our fathers had — they felt richer. Today it is hard it is different. Chimba felt richer I felt smaller — less and less important. He once asked me why it is so — I could not tell him why. I only knew I wanted him to be with me as his wife — no one else. Have you known days and nights when you wanted your man, needed him more than you had ever known it — and he was not there at all? Chimba do you know — do you know what it is like for a woman to feel the children are too much for her they need a father who can talk to them show them the way — children of your own blood Chimba?'

You held me like a python and now I have almost forgotten what it was like. I yearn for something I will never find. You were not there when I needed you Chimba. Since I broke the calabash and your seed went into the ground I feel an emptiness too terrifying to keep my mind on it too deep it has no bottom. First I was grieved when I broke the calabash, then I was relieved that I would not have a new child who would never know the arms and lap of a father — now I feel empty.

'I feel afraid, msuweni, there is a deep fear in this breast. Fear for what I do not know but it is in here. It is the fear I have had from time to time during the lonely days — that I was going to run down the village street with my clothes off and then what would the people think of me? But the fear has deepened into something I cannot name. The first time I knew a fear that I could not do anything about was when Chimba asked me if I would agree to a second wife. He talked like he was joking — perhaps he was — but it left me numb with no warmth in this heart. Then he would not let me help him in his work — even in the days of our forefathers a woman did not just sit around on her buttocks to wait for the man to give her one baby after another. My own peers were marching beside the menfolk in the Copperbelt, they were meeting together to talk and do things to better their lives. I once saw a donkey turning round and round and round to pull a pole that made an engine draw water out of the ground — beating the same path day after day and never complaining. I feared that this was what I would become — the fear of something that will not show its face so that you see it and destroy it — msuweni, that is what I dreaded.

'Chimba O Chimba — we started so well together, we built a home together — our ancestors smiled on us — why would you now go and burn down the house? Were you tired of happiness? You know for yourself msuweni what it means for a wife to have a house she can call her own — even when you have rented it from the town council or from a company you look after it as though it was yours — every woman wants that. For the last four years since Chimba came to the big city my life my children's lives have been restless — never knowing when Chimba was going to send for us. 'He will send for us,' I kept telling his brothers and his father and my father. At last I did not believe my own words anymore — the house we lived in became cold my bed became — oh what is the use? — a woman only knows these things but cannot put them in words — you are a woman yourself msuweni.'

'Were you ever drawn to another man?'

'Oh msuweni, with the Copperbelt so full of men! All those men in the Party — stupid men ugly smelling men some really fine men. One night this friend of our family — we almost did it. I had said many times to myself *why do I have to be the only one to wait and wait and wait when I need Chimba?* I had already heard stories about Chimba in the big city — so that night — when we were undressing I slumped on the bed with my petticoat on — I felt as if something was crawling up my throat — like when you feel you are going to vomit — I felt cheap, as if I was handling smelling dirt — I did not know whether I loved this man so much — I know I grew to love him — but this night I did not know whether it was strong enough or whether it was because my body was aching for a man or whether I was simply hurting myself in the act of trying to free myself to break loose. I told him I could not do it — I cannot do it, I told him. I can never forget that face full of pain as he — as he held my wet face between his hands — I knew then how much he loved me — he was not one of those idiots who dash all over the place working for the Party and think every woman's thighs are the property of the nation. After he left and each time I saw him afterwards — always kind and generous — I threw myself around, beat the wall and the bed with my hands until they hurt. Because I thought Chimba was trampling me down and yet there I was dreading to do the thing that would release me and to do it with a decent man — there I was with Chimba's face always in my mind — a face and eyes that seem always to be threatening and warning you. Often I asked myself how much I loved Chimba, how much I feared him, how much he overpowered me. When he held me like a python I could never tell. But I decided to wait — you know what it is to wait msuweni — if I waited and then pushed him to the point where he would have to take us to the city or else deny us.'

'Let me make some tea for you msuweni.'
'I want to make it msuweni.'
'No, you must rest — you came to my house to rest — would you like some bread and jam?'
'Yes, I thank you msuweni.'
Nsato, the python coiled round a goat... Woman and child fall back and watch, dumbstruck — frightened, stunned by the swift movement of a giant — king of the reptiles. The goat bleating as it will always do when in trouble — but this kind of bleating, helpless and final, is something you can never forget. Ma, Ma, I am afraid! Do not be afraid my child, it is nothing —this is how the ancestors will have it — when you see him you are looking at one of our ancestors. I look at Mother — she speaks as if she is not in control of her tongue — she is looking at the python squeeze the life out of the animal. Her arms round me are trembling — there on the sandy path that the goats have turned into powder with their hoofs. You cannot wait to see how he swallows the animal, Mother says, let us go. Her voice barely above a whisper. She almost drags me behind her as she takes quick strides homeward. We pick up the bundles of firewood where we left them before. Mother's illness — her long long illness. I have never been so frightened before, father-of-Tirenje, never, Mother says, Father tries one herb after another, one doctor follows upon the heels of another, rattles and scatters bones to divine the disease, leaves his herbs... The return to Musoro, to nurse Mother — Mother wasting away. Not everybody sees nsato — when you see him stay away from him. Only if you dare... nsato, the death of a mother... an ancestor visiting death upon us. The last preg-

nancy — carrying the child of Chimba Chirundu. Nsato again, in full view of a woman sitting on the bank of a stream — nsato bathing in the stream — the colossus twisting and coiling down there. I am not afraid of you nsato I am no longer afraid of you — you are an ancestor — if you want to speak to me give me a sign I will listen — my mother has gone to join you — things are as they must be. I am carrying a life in my belly — I am weak I am lonely — oh how alone. Perhaps that is why I am not afraid. I must see you in your full length and bigness so that I may never be afraid as Mother was. Tell me — was it your wish to take her from us in the manner you did? I can feel this life kicking inside me but I must see you wash and go home — I am not afraid anymore, not of you — but I fear the days in front of me — I fear that I shall not have the strength to carry this life until it sees a bright new day if I break this calabash forgive me the gods of Mirimba son of Chisala son of Lilongwe . . . Oh Chimba why did you have to burn down the house we had begun to build — why did you go and fight Hackett and your father only to burn down our house and go build a new one with someone else — is she so much better than me? The day you first took me in your room at school you held me like nsato and nights after that I felt safe in your coils — yes, sometimes a little frightened to see you grow away from me and the children about your business for the nation — but I felt safe and I refused to believe that you would want more than me — I refused to think upon it, upon the stories I later heard. And then you went and burned down our little house . . . Has the python gone mad because of a long time of hunger? Gone mad because he is full of himself?

'And now we can drink our tea msuweni.'

'I am grateful msuweni.'

'Do you not love Chimba any longer?'

'How many times have I asked myself that question? Each time I have said to myself yes —'

'But not enough to share him with another woman.'

'Too much to bear thinking of him sleeping with another woman.'

'Even if he lived only with you he would still seek out another woman you know that.'

'I know it. But it must not be with my consent.'

'Are you afraid you would look yourself in the mirror and think low of yourself — like a woman who has never been to school — I mean the reason that you refused to live with a man of two houses?'

'You are asking me a difficult question msuweni.'

'I have not been to school beyond primary school myself. But I would not allow myself to be a second wife — I am asking a question I would not be able to answer myself.'

'We are living in different times — I do not know — I am not sure why marriages should be different, I just feel times are not the same.'

'Times have always been different — it may be women become more and more vain in every succeeding age.'

'Especially for those who have been to school.'

'Or live in town.'

'What about this other woman? Why would she agree to two houses?'

'She considers herself more important for Chimba in his position, so she can let you live nearby and it will not matter — but the day she felt you were becoming more important her teeth and claws would show.'

'Are you saying I did not try to show that I am more important for Chimba?'

'I do not know.'

'Bringing him to court is my way of showing that I should matter to him — he can then decide which of us he wants more. Which is why I did not simply ask him to divorce me.'

'Who told you about bigamy as a crime?'

'Town folk talk about these things. Then you go to a lawyer to find out the truth.'

'Would you go back to Chimba if he left the other woman?'

'I would.'

'I will tell him this — I will — and try to get him to stop this foolishness.'

'Yes, yes msuweni — you are wise, he may listen to you.'

'But government people never want to think that they made a mistake, do not raise your hopes too high.'

'Has Chimba ever talked to you about me?'

'The few times I have seen him in the city — "I love her I love her and the children," he keeps on saying — but I do not know I do not know with government people, rich people. Us children of the people admire the power they have but we are also afraid they can hurt us, I do not know.'

'Like *nsato*.'

'What? What do you say?'

'I said like *nsato* — but I am not afraid of him anymore. I could go and burn his house down. I can smoke him out — no, he cannot hold me in his coils. I saw him bathing in the stream and I was not afraid.'

'Are you all right msuweni? What are these things you are saying?'

'I am well msuweni do not worry yourself about me. It hurts — here in my breast, the pain only the person you love can give you. It hurts until I want my chest to burst open to drain the poison to ease the pain. Sometimes it is a pain in the head sometimes I feel as if there was a large hole inside me an empty hole that throws back your voice when you try to speak into it.'

'I will speak to Chimba, I will go with you to court tomorrow before he stands up to speak for himself.'

'Sometimes I think I could not go back to him or take him back for the way he treated me, sometimes I think I can for the love I bear for him, sometimes I am afraid again —'

'I will speak to Chimba. If that young man his nephew comes to-night as he promised I will tell him to ask Chimba to meet me at the court before he goes in to speak for himself. This is what we have come to — you have to ask your own blood cousin if you can see him, your own-own msuweni.'

'That last year at Kapiri, msuweni — in secondary school I was taught by a young woman — what was her name? — Elena — Elena Mwansa — that was 1954. I was seventeen. I would never have thought at the time that what Elena Mwansa said to us would have so much direct meaning for me and my life with Chimba. A slender woman with deep black shining eyes — she was the first woman to take the B.A. — in the whole country — she got it in South Africa — the famous college for Africans there. Fourteen years ago and still her words ring in my mind today. "Stand up and do things for yourselves and your people," she said. "You are the women of tomorrow. I have seen African women in South Africa — the people of the land — those from Rhodesia, Uganda, Mozambique, Bechuanaland, Basutoland. They are awake and our women are still sitting under trees here because the white man has taken much of the land. Listen to me, my students," Elena Mwansa told us, "listen to me — those people down there in the south also lost their lands, but they do not sit gaping at the sun — they cook food and brew beer to sell — good beer that is as good as food. They go out to the factories, they sew clothes and sell — many things." And then she said, "There are men who will want to marry you in order to use you, do things which even our elders never did — as if suddenly they had got mad with power. My father," Elena Mwansa told us — I can still see her bright shining eyes — she said, "our fathers knew what a woman is worth, where her power lies. But young men of your age, even mine, think that because they call themselves modern, because more women are going to school, more things are open for us to do than there were for our mothers, so more women are also open to men to take and use." Elena Mwansa said also that no man has any use for a woman who has no mind of her own, who cannot know what to do where she is needed. She said the man who wants a woman for a thing to kick about is himself very weak. A strong man wants a strong wife — but a strong woman does not need to put on trousers — there are better ways she can show her strength.'

'Have those wonderful words helped you msuweni?'

'There were times when I took courage from them and there have been times when I wished Elena Mwanza was still alive for me to ask her questions. The poor woman died from a sickness in the lungs — yes msuweni, I cried many such times not knowing where to turn. Chimba became too much for me — Elena's words seemed out of place then, but I knew if Chimba had given me a chance they would have worked. Oh Chimba *why* did you have to burn the house down, why could you not give me a chance? Msuweni, is this the way it was to be, because our men began to make laws, began to control their own country? Was it to be like this?'

'I do not know msuweni — I wish I could give you the answer.'

Knock, knock, knock!
'Mulibwanji?'
'Zikomo ndilibwino.'
'Ndilibwino.'

'It is good to see you mupwa. How is my nephew's business with the workers?'

'They are ready.'

'Before I forget, Moyo, tell your asibweni tonight if you can that I want to talk to him tomorrow morning at the court — before his case begins — can you reach him?'

'I will telephone, mai, I will try.'

'If you cannot tonight I must simply go to the court tomorrow and hold him by the jacket.'

'I brought some food.'

'We thank you.'

'We thank you.'

'Mai wamung'ono, you think you have troubles? Listen to mine —

the good mother here will be my witness — I cannot understand my uncle — he goes about telling bad stories about me. He is older than me and I want to show him due respect — but what am I to say when I hear people in the bars and at work tell me my uncle says I am ungrateful? Look at him — he tells people — that milkbelly of a boy — meaning me — I go and bury his mother and I pay all expenses and I give him a job in my department and what thanks does he give me? Now tell me good mothers — was not my mother his own blood sister? Was he doing mother's children and husband a favour? And just because he helped me to get a job in his department must I stand on the side of the government and not on the side of those with whom I work? Must I accept low wages and other bad things because the Minister is my uncle? Are we all relatives in government? I cannot understand my uncle — please help me good mothers — I do not want to go into a war of words against an older person, uncle or no uncle — that is the way my parents, my grandfather Mutiso, that is the way they taught me. Now what am I to do? I am a worker, the other workers made me secretary. I did not ask for the position.'

'Has he ever talked to you about all this, Moyo?'

'Yes, mai, the night I took a letter to him from my committee to tell him that we shall wait for his case to be over before we go on strike. You see, the prosecutor told us that it would only take a few days. That night he spoke strong words to say that I was still young and should not be misled by others. And do you know who he thinks has poisoned my mind? A man from South Africa — Letanka — who is a teacher at the night school whose class I am attending. Now my uncle sees enemies through every keyhole — a-ah — will you talk to him tomorrow, mai, when you see him. I am his nephew and I cannot cross words with him. Can you tell him, mai, that I feel hurt? I swear by my grandfather Mutiso who is in his grave that I would not do my uncle any personal harm — what I am doing is against the government and he is not the government.'

'That is not the way to speak, mupwa!'

'Why not mai wamung'ono? I am speaking what is in my heart.'

'He is not, but you say it as if he wants to be the government, as if he stood on top of parliament house and shouted *I am the government!* — as if you mean *Chimba must not fancy he is the government.* Do you hear me, mupwa? He is still your uncle and still my husband. Your strike and then this trial — I do not know.'

'Why can you not call mai your msuweni here and my uncle and grandfather Mirimba in Musoro and grandfather Chirundu in Shimoni and talk about this matter?'

'You are too young to understand, mupwa. Your uncle and me have come a long way, a long long way — I can see our house burning down, beams and walls falling down and no one can save it any more.'

'Did you try to call these people before, mai wamung'ono? I asked when you arrived, I asked my uncle after your quarrel with Monde — you told me you had tried, my uncle only kept silent. But even when he was silent I could hear him try to swallow his anger.'

'Give your little mother time to rest, Moyo. Tell your uncle that if he cannot see me before he speaks in court he must come to me soon after. He always has people crawling around him so it will be easier for him to come to me.'

'I will, mother. Sleep well, good people.'

'Tell me, msuweni, what your father and Chimba's father really think about this? You had other relations in the Copperbelt — Chimba's brothers and you must have all talked about it.'

'We did, oh so many times. Chimba told his brothers to mind their own work and to stay out of his affairs. There has seldom been any warmth between him and his father ever since the old man was baptised and drove out his wives — Chimba's mother one of them, Moyo's grand-mother the other one — oh those two men — Chimba and old Chirundu! What made things worse msuweni was that his father was angry at the way he treated Hackett — a man of God — the way we married — after the child was born which was not the way of the church. It was quite clear that even had Chimba been willing to come and meet us all in the house of old Chirundu, they would have fought before they talk-ed and in the stench of it all no one would have spoken sense. The time Chirundu called Chimba to meet us at Shimoni on our way to Musoro the old man had planned to call my father. Is it not right for me to talk to the people of Chirundu, and Chimba to the people of Mirimba when there is trouble of this size in the home?'

'It is, msuweni — that is how we are taught — that is how it should be. I know Chimba is a hard man.'

'Those who knew them tell that the people of Chirundu before Chimba's father were like that. I think old Chirundu is even prepared to forgive them for this. When we were in Shimoni on our way to Musoro he kept hissing and spitting angry words — like *this son of a stiff-necked clan — this son of heathens . . . In one line we have idiots, failures, loaf-ers, pumpkins, drunks, and when we married outside we begot a line of*

*hotheads, bullheads, studs, wilful proud heathens . . . God and the an-
cestors turned their backs on us — and now we have read books too,
eh? — we run the government, eh? and someone thinks he can walk
over people as he would a doormat — burn this house down, build that
one.'*

'What does your father say? '

'They met with Chirundu. They only shook their heads, my father
told me — if Chimba could not appear what could they do? My father
simply said, "Tirenje my child, Tirenje my child, do what you think
will bring you relief from this big weight — you are still thirty years of
age if you want to do it you can still begin another life — this way you
are living you are wasting away — but do what you can to save this marriage — the children need their real father but they cannot have him —
there are many men who would love them as they would their own
blood." '

'And Chirundu?'

'He has never given any advice. My mind has always told me that he
understood and we understood that there could be no divorce — we
married in sin, we could not sin again in order to correct the first one —
God help us in the sin that was always going to bind us together — Chirundu would think that way. The very few times we have met he never
seemed to know what to do with me — he could not look me straight in
the face. The first time we met I feared the old man would simply tell
Chimba to take this woman out of his house — from what his son had
told me I could not imagine it any other way.'

'How could he msuweni? A person's father-in-law is hers whether
they both like it or not.'

'My father came to visit us in Luanshya and stopped to see Chirundu.
My father told us the story of their argument. I am surprised you could
give your daughter to that heathen son of mine, he says to my father.
But it was his brothers who came to Musoro to ask for her. My friend,
father tells him, even had you wanted Tirenje to be the one to gladden
your heart with grandchildren, you know that you would not be
allowed by the law of the elders to bring yourself to my house — I
would not receive you, I would send you back as a badly brought-up
old man. Chirundu replies, he says, you are right, friend, although I am
a Christian I would not want to offend the ancestors. Indeed, father
says, even if you felt here inside your heart that your sons were not
voicing your desire it would not matter — your son would still have
taken Tirenje. *They did not marry like children of Christian families,*

Chirundu roars aloud. *For that I ask God to forgive them, I cannot myself forget it!* You know what father says? He tells Chirundu, Tirenje has not married *you* and neither has Chimba married me — what you and I think will add nothing to the marriage, take nothing from it — and now here I am drinking all this bottle of whisky, which I brought for us to share, because you became a Christian — you say to me God will not allow it. Father goes on to say to him, he says, what an unhappy God you have made for yourself! You know, this is one of the bottles Chimba brought me when we had that party for them at Musoro — and you sat there chewing sweets! And my father laughs as he tells us this.'

'Chirundu must think now that God's judgment is on your heads because you married outside the church?'

'That is just what he said to me. That gave me pain.'

I wanted us to talk Chimba seek out each other's hearts listen to them and you stayed out of reach what was it that made you take me into your arms and come into me a mere schoolgirl that afternoon in Kapiri?

'Greetings msuweni!'
'Greetings msuweni Chimba!'
'Tirenje! Greetings! Mulibwanji?'
'Greetings Chimba!'
'Zikomo ndilibwino — mulibwanji?'
Chimba! How much darker you look, how much deeper your eyes have sunken in!

'All right. Msuweni, I met Moyo at their offices. Says you want to see me. Impossible tomorrow — I've a little time this evening — but only a little.'

'We are eating.'

'I thank you, I cannot stay long msuweni — but eat, I will wait.'

So you are never going to come back to me Chimba? You will not even talk to me as your wife . . .

'I forget that you high people eat better food and you sit at table.'

'You're teasing me again, msuweni — let me have a little pumpkin and stop feeling pity for yourself.'

'Let us go into my bedroom and we can talk while we eat.'

'I shall stay here and eat.' *You will not even look me straight in the eyes Chimba. But you stand erect still . . . I do not know that suit — did she buy it for you? — these town women buy presents for men . . . the* suit must be from London as always . . . your servant washes your shirts well too — I used to do them myself . . . So you will not come back Chimba . . . I want you back . . . this trial is only a fight to get you back if you choose to return. I am not the drifter, I am still where you left me . . . but I shall not always be there . . . What do I read on that dark face in those deep eyes — distaste? defeat, surrender? worry? triumph? or just the plain stonewilled manner of Chirundu people . . . (I can hear loud words from that room). Take care Tirenje walk slowly do not make a fool of yourself not more than you have already — you thought things could be talked over . . . Would you really take him back if he made the choice yours? A man who has been into another woman — not just a stray mare waiting for any rider but a woman who aims to own him, keep him . . . You know what a man said to my father when I was a girl? When I told him about Chimba's woman he said he knew this man who had come back from the mines in Johannesburg who used to tell him after a few calabashes of beer that a city woman is like a road — when you come to it it is foolish to ask who has walked here before — more than that, just bear in mind also that someone else may come and walk there after you. (What is he saying in such a loud voice in there?) Is that how you think of yourself msuweni? I can believe it — you are a widow but I am sure — I can see it — you know how to overcome loneliness . . . A woman turns into a goatpath because she is afraid of loneliness . . . Something has touched us who live in the city or have read books at school — some strange magic — or it is as if we were caught in a net and ripped away from the teachings of our elders and now loneliness comes easy to us . . . Father says to keep with people is to know who you are where you come from and you can carry the pain of your loneliness . . . In the Copperbelt there were so many people — I could carry it although I felt it . . . at Musoro, many women and men my age have gone the land is unable to feed them, oh what loneliness . . . Something strange has touched us in the white man's school and church, in the white man's town and we make loneliness in our selves as the factory makes clothes — so I heard Chimba say once . . . Is this what you meant Chimba — is that what you would say of Tirenje's loneliness even though she is not alone? Where does msuweni find her strength? So you will not come back Chimba! Are you also lonely? (what is he saying that needs to be shouted?) Save yourself Tirenje, save yourself and the children.

'She will come back if you want her msuweni Chimba.'

'If she wanted that she would not have got that big Che Chimimba to drag me into court!'

'She thought the case would bring you down from the top, make you know her again as the only woman for you. She believed you could not see her as a better woman as long as you sat so high in government.'

'WHY NOT DIVORCE ME INSTEAD OF DISGRACING ME LIKE THIS — A MAN IN MY POSITION! —'

'Sh! Not loud, do you want her to hear you? Have you become blind Chimba? Do you not see that if she divorced you she would lose you? The only way she could claim you would be to put you in a place where the law would prevent you keeping two wives, you would then have to say to yourself *Chimba, which woman do you love most?* Tirenje told me herself. If you lost the power of a man of government you would ask the question sooner and answer it quicker.'

'If I still decide to keep Monde after the trial?'

'She will know she has failed — but she would also be saved from the pain of divorcing someone she still loves, because it would be *your* problem to start the divorce.'

'TIRENJE HAD THE CHANCE TO MAKE OUR KIND OF MAR—RIAGE WORK. SHE MAKES TROUBLE AND AS SOME PEOPLE SAY, FUCKS UP!'

'Shshsh! No language like that in my house Chimba you hear me!'

'I am sorry.'

'Are you prepared to lose the children?'

'Yes, only for a while. I will be responsible for them and they will grow up to know I am their father.'

'You wanted two wives, eh?'

'Yes I wanted two wives.'

'In these days — in the nineteen sixties? An educated man, a man of government? Or are you so drunk with money you do not know what to do with it? Why not throw what you do not need to your poor cousin who has to mend even a cheap petticoat?'

'You have no cause to complain. Your husband left you a paid-up house, you can lease part of it and live on the money with no need to work.'

'I would still have to work as I am working now. You are not going to drive me from the subject of the marriage. Remember as your cousin I am aunt to your children and you are not a Minister in my house. You are just a son of Chirundu, who should have had better sense than to send you to school.'

'I am a self-made man msuweni — left to himself Chirundu would have sent me to the Copperbelt to work in the mines.'

'You keep running away from the real matter.'

'My mind is made up.'

'You are going to carry through this moment? And the strike?'

'We are ready for trouble. Those country bumpkins who have just arrived in town and are already messing with big stuff like a strike — they'll know their place. I'm quite capable of taking them on while I sort out my home troubles.'

'That reminds me of your nephew Moyo.'

'*That* one! What is it with him?'

'He has asked me to talk to you — he respects you and does not want to trade hard words with his uncle. He says he hears stories around in places that matter that you accuse him of being ungrateful — you buried his mother and gave him a job and now he is leading a strike against you.'

'I've spoken to other people about it, yes, but he cannot complain that I have been talking behind his back — I accused him to his face.'

'You believe he is doing this to spite you?'

'I believe no less.'

'He is still young msuweni and full of spirits — but he is only one of many workers — are you going to deny him — the way your father tried to push you out of his mind?'

'My father's case is different. Indeed I could almost forgive him. This from Moyo is a direct stab in the back — THE LITTLE BILLYGOAT STRUTTING ABOUT FULL OF THE SMELL OF HIMSELF — PERHAPS BECAUSE HE CAN GROW A BEARD!'

'Chimba, you are foolhardy — indeed stupid! Why do you persist in hurting yourself, in telling dark clouds to shut off the sun so that it does not bring warmth into your heart? Why do you want to act like a small man who cannot fight because he has a withered hand or a twisted leg?'

'This is a national matter — what I care for or do not care for is not important — THOSE COUNTRY BUMPKINS ARE GOING TO EAT DUNG!'

'No such language in my house!'

'I tell you we're ready — they'll be eating grass and dung the second day of their strike!'

'You are foolhardy — I still say so Chimba — if you do not bend you will break.'

'I like you msuweni and I respect you, so do not spoil that! The matter is closed.'

'Still talking like a Minister eh? The ancestors will settle scores with you — I want them to punish you until you see light and come down on your knees and beg for mercy — but I fear it will be too late for anybody else's good. That daughter of the people in there needs you, your children need you — they are not a national concern are they? — any other woman would have been fighting you all the way, she would have come to shout at you in your offices, she would have dumped the children in your own office. Tell me son of Chirundu — just tell me the full truth — would you have enjoyed letting Tirenje keep a man during all those lonely days and nights — would you?'

'Of course not, woman! She is my wife.'

'And you would not want her to say Chimba is my husband and no one else's?'

'It's not the same thing IT'S NOT THE SAME THING!'

'No, it is not the same thing, it will never be the same thing until Chimba the son of Chirundu will have it so. I have finished. You will want to talk to her — I shall stay here and —'

'No! I thought I would but —'

'Shsh! Yes — you shall — she is still your wife.'

'Tirenje.'

'You have finished?'

'Yes.'

'Do you want us to talk, Chimba?'

'Yes, do you?'

'Msuweni must have told you —'

'Tirenje, we are not children.'

'She told you my feelings?'

'Yes.'

'Your answer?'

'It will not work — this trial has poisoned the air everywhere I breathe.'

'You think it has been a time of ripe corn and melons and sugar cane and festival for me and the children?'

'I am sorry you lost the child.'

'You see it only as my loss?'

'You know I do not mean it that way. How are the children?'

'How can I say of children who have not known a father's love long — that they are happy and healthy?'

'You know it was not only my doing that has brought us to this.'

'I did not burn a house down and leave for another man.'

'You knew everything I was doing — I concealed nothing.'

'No Chimba — you did so well that you thought nothing of throwing me into the same house with that woman to see if we would fight over you —'

'Not a word more about her — I did not come here to talk about her! I did not put you in the same house — you —'

'Two wives in the same town is like two wives in the same house — you said a few moments ago that we are not children — are you going to come back to the burnt down house and then say you were not to blame because you only wanted the roof on fire?'

'I gave you a chance to try my plan for two houses because you wanted to come to the city.'

'Would you have taken a divorce?'

'It would have been better than this.'

'But either way I could not hope to continue to be your wife — is that it?'

'You tried my plan — it did not work — you want to be my only wife, which is impossible. So we are wasting time trading bitter words like this. My lawyer will meet you in court tomorrow to arrange how the money can be sent every month for you and the children — I shall be generous — do not worry about that. This is necessary when people divorce — I believe you want a divorce as the case is bound to be in your favour?'

'It is you who wants a divorce Chimba — so you do what you like. You know, I used to think of myself as a boulder that a man would always find where he left it. I was wrong — I got to learn that the bitter way. A boulder takes anything you splash on it and gives nothing. A woman gives. And then I thought the joy is only in the giving. I got to learn that it lay in the giving and the taking. You are now telling me you have no need of me — indeed you began to abandon the home when you went into politics — that is as you wished. Your father drove out two wives — one of them your own mother —'

'Stop there — just you stop there — don't — don't talk about my father, about my father — what I have done — what I have done has nothing to do with his life — you hear me — you hear me?'

'It has come to the same thing — you have burned down a house — I saw the flames and could not stop the fire — perhaps tomorrow another house will go down in flames and yet another be put up.'

'No such thing will happen — you are out of your mind — Monde will always be with me.'

'In the new house, which I have not even dared to see from the outside?'

'Yes — can you not understand?'

'One last wish Chimba — when I die — wherever it may be — do not come to my funeral. People have a way of throwing out a person and then trooping to her funeral as if they were going to pick her bones — as if to make sure she is not trying to make trouble again — *nsato* will watch over the grave, so do not even dare to bring flowers — you hear me well Chimba! Your children you can collect if they are not living their own lives — they are still of Chirundu blood.'

'You are strong enough — you are not going to die for a long long time — I don't know why you want to be pitied — it will not change anything.'

'You think I want pity? Hm — do you sound like a man who had any grain of it to give? Pity? How little you know me. We did not know each other when we met in that school of Kapiri and we part still knowing nothing. One thing though, I feel I have grown in mind twenty years ahead of you although you are five years older than me.'

'Sleep well Tirenje! I AM OFF — MSUWENI.'

'Go in peace msuweni.'

'CHIMBAAAAAAAA!'

'Calm yourself msuweni.'

'Tell me from where you are standing — I must know this instant —'

'Yes, Tirenje — I am listening.'

'Have you stopped loving me?'

'Why do you ask me this tonight?'

'Well — have you?'

'There was a time when the question would have been a big thing — now it is not any longer.'

'Thank you for no answer.' *I see the flames leaping into the sky of the night and I cannot do anything to stop it — there is nsato, leaping in the air finding no way out of the flames — he is writhing and thrashing and leaping and smashing down the beams and the glass on himself — how can anyone be so cruel as to burn an ancestor — who is so cruel, cruel . . . My children . . . I need you so much but you are so far away . . . Father, they are your grandchildren . . . Teach them not to fear nsato . . . whether he comes as the great good ancestor or the wicked ancestor who waylays the woodgatherer and the traveller . . .*

'It is time for bed msuweni.'
'Yes, it is time, daughter of the people.'

Studs: When do you think you'll go back?

Pitso: Any day now. I want to be so sure that I don't change my mind on the way.

Chieza: Will you tell this man that he's committing suicide — you don't come out of jail so as to go back in!

Studs: See, I didn't come out as a refugee, I left for other reasons. I can still go and visit my mother. I can understand Pitso's longing. Man, I feel that longing to teach among my own people sweep through me like a flood, man, and I feel I'm drowning. And yet I know I won't do what is most natural. To go in there is to go against authority and then the bloodhounds come at you.

Chieza: These South Africans! One moment I think I understand you, the next moment I don't see you clearly. They'll break you, those Boers.

Pitso: I'll survive. So Moyo's strike is hotting up eh?

Studs: That's how Chirundu sees it — Moyo's strike, not the Transport workers.

Chieza: Hei, he's appearing this morning.

Studs: Stupid case.

Pitso: What the fellow did was stupid, not the case.

Studs: 'T's what I mean — the whole tin can rattle.

Chieza: Think they'll fry the Portuguese spies?

Studs: Who knows? Any day now they'll come up for trial. About the strike — I was going to say Moyo's uncle is mad at him — thinks Moyo's betraying the family — lining up the strikers' cannons against him personally — just when he has this bigamy circus on. Guess what also? I'm supposed to have taught Moyo everything — trade union movement, methods of subverting labour, the lot.

Pitso: These small-time politicians! Soon he'll be pushing you out of the country.

Studs: Possible, but he's too busy with other things right now.

Chieza: What — an international organization!

Studs: The worst the host country can do is discredit you and have you transferred.

Chieza: This Transport coon — what'll he get — two years, or will he be let off with a fine?

Studs: It's reckoned this is the kind of case that does not carry a fine, and of course he knows he's guilty. Certificates are there to show it.

Pitso: What the fuckin' hell's he defending himself for — is it a political game? And why is he not suspended?

Studs: You've answered your own question.

Chieza: Hear me hear me sons of Africa, when I am in power I'll have me a bunch of beauties scattered all over — town thighs and country thighs — get me a chauffeur to drive me to each.

Pitso: The stud you are, you could round up five in a single night. I wonder you can stay here and refuse to return to Zimbabwe for the girls.

Chieza: And what about our comrades there from Angola and Namibia? Should we all get our asses shot up even before we meet the first woman? YOU'RE GOING TO GET YOUR ASS SHOT UP, SON OF AFRICA!

Pitso: If that happens it'll still be better than this dump. At least it will have been because I was trying to better my situation. Here people have to shuffle papers on your behalf while you go through this fuckin' *kwacha* routine from that halfwit.

Studs: No need to get worked up about it brother. I always say save your energy for the real ordeal. As I see it we are faced with a variety of problems all at once: there's no one answer to them. Independence found Africa loaded with whole systems that our people had to keep if they were to function immediately, keep the services going. Many of the systems are new to Africa, some are not wanted. I mean there's Jesus Christ, there's Mohammed, there are laws, rites that the Christian white man ruled the natives by. What's all this got to do with a Cabinet Minister who lays two women and decides to keep them both as wives?

Our fathers and their fathers before them kept more than one wife, they flourished. Here comes a man who trips up on British law that says you cannot own more than one wife under an Ordinance handed down in writing by our British fathers. Their Christian church condemned our fathers' customs.

Chieza: Then the coon should have avoided British law altogether, just taken two wives under the law of his fathers.

Studs: The one who brought about this case would not have it that way.

Pitso: Why didn't she leave him?

Studs: I don't know all the facts of the quarrel — who can, ever, if you're not in it? — but she wanted to keep him and hoped she'd win eventually, that the second woman would be fired.

Chieza: Which didn't happen. So she suffers.

Studs: The law will never be repealed and so people will keep concubines — *that's* a system for you! Look at the trade union movement: what does a worker do who finds that the politicians who were the backbone of the unions, and used them too for a broad national front for self-rule — what does a worker do when he finds after independence that the same politicians, now in government, resent his demands for better working conditions and wages? What does he do when he's accused of being irresponsible, of subverting the cause of nation building? See what Chirundu is a product of?

Pitso: Are you saying his behaviour is predetermined and he can do nothing to stop the troubles he's in?

Studs: Maybe he had excessive confidence in what his political power could do for him. A man of your standing or mine could hardly commit bigamy because you have nothing to protect you. Right now he must be trying to wield that power in court. Remember that ugly thing — 1966 — with the Minister of Education when his black American wife was deported? The plane could hardly have landed in Rome before he took a wife from his own ethnic group — oh well, a short time afterwards anyway. Comes to the same thing because he found it necessary to correct a newspaper report that captioned a picture of the two at an official party 'Mr F R Muli and companion enjoying a joke with the German ambassador' etcetera etcetera. Instructed the reporter to say Mrs Muli instead of 'his companion' next time. The reporter himself told me — and that was less than two weeks after the deportation.

Chieza: What kind of woman is Tirenje? — you've seen her.

Studs: A few times. Two women could not be more different than

Chirundu's. This one — Tirenje — is firmly built, compact — you know — not flabby. She has a firm stride, stands on strong legs. A well-rounded bosom that you want to press against you — you know — you want to bury your head between those breasts and listen to an ancient story from deep down there. The face was once round, but I am sure it has been weathered some by loneliness and grief. And yet the eyes are still steady, they look you straight in the face, as if they were telling you of something vital in the woman that can never be destroyed. No make up, understand? Just plain commonsense good looks handed down by the gods . . . Braids her hair and puts on a headcloth when she goes out. You look at her and you are contented to know Africa still makes them — her kind.

Chieza: Watchit Studs, watchit man, you speak too much from the heart for your own good. The other woman?

Studs: Well now, there's another bundle. Frankly I don't know what to make of her. But the two are different. Monde appears at a cocktail — you know, the kind of do government big shots put on to show how far they've ee-merged. Anyhow she moves in as if this social element was made for her, as if she had ordered it. And yet she doesn't thrust herself — no, man — she doesn't have to. You've got to give it to that Chirundu boy — he's no fool, he's discriminating. I mean most of these government boys have concubines they daren't exhibit in public, so they don't have to look for particularly pretty women for their extramural games. But this Chirundu boy says I'm going to have two wives and they must both be presentable. Only — only — of course — the city one is more at ease in the atmosphere set up by this brittle and precious group — all this glitter — I mean this atmosphere the entertainment machine of government can reproduce with the bang of a rubber stamp — know what I mean?

Chieza: You'd do the same thing if you were in power of course.

Studs: What you talkin', man — I would — I do go because I'm invited and I like cocktail parties — free drinks and you can observe faces — the same you've seen dozens of times before — but *you* are looking differently each time. Hell, you realize what's happening? — I take so long trying to tell you about Monde like I was seeing a reflection of her in water — or maybe like I was seeing her through window glass on a rainy day. The headcloth, the Congo-style dress, the slender body, small eyes set wide apart — kind of distance you don't usually associate with an alert mind.

Pitso: Hei, she studied in England, right?

Studs: Ya. Well — wide mouth, nose that doesn't stand out like Tirenje's, powdered face, pencilled brows, dark lips — almost indigo — that's all I remember of her. I just don't know what to make of her — she's a difficult script, man, tough. You look at the other wife and you feel you'd get somewhere with her if you took your time — I mean you could go slowly over each line a few times to understand the script and the line would still be there for you to come back to. And then there is the depth you don't immediately sense looking at Monde.

Chieza: You think Tirenje couldn't fit into this kind of crowd — I mean you couldn't then be saying that Chirundu needs different wives for different functions?

Studs: How the hell can I know? We in the south went through a destructive system — migrant labour — we also lost our land and we were shoved around from one part of the territory to another. Then the system of education *plus* Christian teaching drummed into our skulls an image of man as a one-wife animal, and economic pressures did the rest.

Pitso: Same as here — wouldn't you say? — everywhere the Europes have set foot.

Studs: Sure, only — over a longer time in the south — more intensively too because of greater industrialization — consider seven million urban blacks as against the mostly rural populations in other African countries. I never judge people according to what I think is right or wrong, — hell, man — *whose* idea of right or wrong — the white man's? — in matters like these I do what my instincts tell me, within the limits of reason. Chirundu wanted to keep two wives in a respectable way — consider *that* — he didn't want to go sneaking in and out of concubines at night or have sometimes to fly out through the concubine's window without pyjamas on — how can I put it? — dramatic nights — you know — those nights when you find yourself in a triangle.

Chieza: Call them triangular nights.

Pitso: Oh noooh!

Studs: No, he wanted respectable bigamy, but bigamy is an English word that is loaded with English Christian culture and it's by definition non-respectable. And from what Moyo tells me, Tirenje was not unsuited or unprepared for this sort of life. She was hostess full-time to lots of people who went in and out of their house in the Copperbelt — all political types — only it was a mixed crowd — coarse and genteel, town and rural people, old and young, illiterate and otherwise.

Chieza: So she would need to polish her style a bit, eh? I mean to deal with a select group at a level of high life.

Studs: That would be easy for a woman of her background.

Chieza: Hei, you seem to admire this fellow Chirundu — you sympathize with him so much.

Studs: I don't know if I sympathize with him — or pity him. I think it's pity I feel. I'm trying to understand him in order that I might understand — what? Maybe the things that have happened to us — since the Europes came to this continent. What a big fat lie we educated folks are living — and we dare not make the choices we must — because they are difficult, awkward or unpractical, or premature; or because they will remind us who we are and demand that we go through the whole process of tearing up and reconstructing parts of the system. People make excuses because they are too lazy or bankrupt of ideas or too sold on the Europes, too comfortable to act as a body or nation. So the individuals who make the choices look like radicals, trouble makers, they don't realize we need time to consolidate independence first — blah — blah — blah. So the law deals with them. The rest of the nation regard them as tedious, silly deviates. The boys in power tell the people not to make trouble — not to harass them in the great work of nation building. They tell labourers not to strike and disturb the economy — it's unpatriotic.

Pitso: You could hardly call Chirundu a radical, could you?

Chieza: Hau!

Studs: No, not a political radical. But a radical of some sort who is trying to shake a social code people have always taken for granted.

Chieza: Think he's using this as a defence?

Studs: We'll know when *Nation Times* comes out this evening.

Warder (from the door): Kwacha! One country one nation! Time up! In the name of the President, Chief of Defence, Chief Justice, Chief of Prisons, I must tell you that it is time up! Kwacha!

Pitso: Poor chap — he still insists that he's an employee of the Ministry of Defence — says prisons are part of the defence force.

Studs: Aren't they? Peace, comrades! Moyo's too busy to come, but you'll see me.

Chieza: Tell Moyo we wish him well. If the new day has deceived the Chirundus, the Moyos of this land may yet move to a brighter dawn.

Pitso: Peace, old boy!

MOYO

April 4, morning

Defence Counsel, Mr Clare, opens his case.

You are the accused in this case?

Yes, I am.

Do you know Tirenje Chirundu, née Mirimba?

Yes, I do.

Was she your wife before?

Yes.

How were you married?

First by Bemba law, then under the Ordinance. The former was registered at a Boma.

Did you get a certificate for this?

No. I did not.

What happened next?

I went through another marriage, this time under the marriage Ordinance.

Why did you find it necessary to marry again?

I did so to please my first wife.

I see, she was not happy that you did not give her a certificate?

That is true.

You then got a certificate?

Yes.

This is what she wanted?

Yes, she was now happy.

Was your marriage with Tirenje Mirimba a happy one?

At the beginning yes. Recently things went wrong.

Will you explain what happened?

I wanted a woman who could measure up to my social and political status, but I still loved Tirenje, so I arranged for her to come and join us in the capital.

Did she come?

Yes, but she could not put up with it and she left for her father's house in Musoro, Eastern Province.

Did you maltreat her?

Not at all.

Why, when you had married her under the Ordinance did you not divorce her and then remarry?

I loved her too much to do that. *(Hisses and sniggers in the court.)*

Are you now married to Monde Lundia?

Yes.

How?

Under the Ordinance. *(Louder hisses and exclamations in the court. The judge cautions the people.)*

Were you not aware that you were committing bigamy since your first marriage under the Ordinance was still in force?

No. Because I considered the traditional customary law under which I first married Tirenje still valid.

Why did you not keep Tirenje, then, under that law?

Because according to tradition her people should have contacted me for discussions once she left me to return to Musoro. They did not.

Were you satisfied in your mind that there was nothing to prevent you marrying Monde Lundia?

Yes.

The case for the defence rests, my Lord.

Do you want to cross-examine, Mr Wanika?

As your Lordship pleases. Mr Chirundu, are you a stranger to the truth?

Why? That's an insult, your Lordship!

I must ask you to answer questions from the State Advocate directly, Mr Chirundu, not to comment on the nature of the questions.

You've heard what his Lordship has said.

I am sorry, Sir.

Continue, Mr Wanika.

As your Lordship pleases. Mr Chirundu, will you answer my question — are you a stranger to the truth?

I am not answering the question — it's got nothing to do with this case.

I see. Is it or is it not true that when you visited the Boma in Kapiri on 4 November 1959 in order to get married the marriage officer explained to you the consequences of contracting a second marriage under the Ordinance when a former one was subsisting?

Yes. The former one happened to be by customary law.

And he told you that a person can only take one wife or one husband at a time under the Marriage Ordinance, and you were subsequently told this again by the marriage officer?

Yes.

So you deliberately perjured yourself on the occasion of your second marriage in 1968 by concealing the fact that your 1959 marriage under the Ordinance still subsisted?

That is an academic question because I still recognized my contract under native and customary law as valid. *(The judge warns the accused that if he makes comments a third time he will charge him with contempt of court.)*

Mr Chirundu, do you mean to sit there and tell this respectable court that you, an educated man and a Cabinet Minister could (a) not know that you were contracting an illicit marriage in 1968 and (b) that you could not see that the officer's recital of the law implied that if it was relevant to your case you should stop what you were doing, (c) that you were signing an affidavit you did not understand? *(Loud noises and sniggers in the court. The judge instructs the court to be cleared except for the parties and witnesses involved in the trial and the newspapermen. The court is cleared.)*

I still regarded my marriage as valid under customary law and the Ordinance did not matter any more.

Why then did you not contract your second marriage by both laws so that in future if you wanted to marry again — especially since your first wife was for all intents and purposes out of your life — you could again stand on Bemba law?

I cannot answer that. Can't a man use these instruments as and when he wants?

I shall overlook that high-school debating stunt and put it to you that you took advantage of your official position and authority to flout the law!

I will not answer that.

No, not *will not*, Mr Chirundu — *cannot*. Did you not sign an affidavit when you married in 1959 and 1968 declaring that you were not married under the Ordinance before?

I did.

Why, if you knew you were perjuring yourself in 1968?

I still honour and respect customary law which comes from our ancestors.

Even though you are aware that the Marriage Ordinance supersedes customary law?

Yes.

That is the end of my cross-examination, my Lord.

Any re-examination, Mr Clare?

No re-examination, my Lord.

(The judge takes off his glasses and addresses the accused.)

Your marriage certificate for 1959 describes you as a quote Politician unquote, and in the 1968 one you are described as a quote Minister of Transport and Public Works unquote. Do you still function in the latter capacity?

Yes, my Lord.

How far did you go in school?

As far as teacher training, my Lord.

Did you practice your profession?

Yes, my Lord.

Did you go for any further studies?

No, my Lord.

How long did you teach?

Five years.

Thank you. Any questions, Mr Clare?

No questions, my Lord.

Mr Wanika?

No further questions, my Lord.

Will the accused go back to the dock. Will you sum up for the prosecution, Mr Wanika?

The State Advocate alternately puts his pudgy fingers in the waistcoat pocket and plays with one of the buttons. He speaks. First marriage . . . second marriage . . . bigamy . . . deliberate bigamy committed by someone with a reasonable education — a member of Government — who has delusions about his ancestors, as he calls them . . . This man, my Lord, has a lot to hide . . . The witnesses have come up with damning evidence . . . I will ask the Court to find that the accused is a very intelligent man and cannot be forgiven for simplemindedness in the one-man crusade he thinks he is staging against the law of the country . . . if he wants to change it, he knows what statutory measures to take . . . he cannot be allowed to continue in a reckless career of breaking women's hearts and leaving them desolate. I shall therefore ask the Court to find the accused guilty as charged . . .

Defence Counsel moves in. The accused has been candid in declaring his motives . . . He does not deny marrying the two women . . . he honestly believed, on reasonable grounds, that at the time of his second marriage his former contract had been dissolved under Bemba law. On the authority of Gould (1963) it is enough that such reasonable grounds did exist, without reference to the question as to whether or not the accused did in fact have such honest belief and that it was based on reasonable grounds . . . Accused has shown that Bemba law brings customary marriages to an end under certain conditions, and has shown that these conditions did exist in the present case . . . This area of the law, which easily lends itself to conflict between Western conceptions and African traditional conceptions, has to be approached with particular sympathy for those who are exposed to culture conflicts. I think the law has to accept the fact that although institutions may change overnight . . . the ultimate values of society take a great deal of time to evolve and transform . . . In this case we are faced with a situation where the quote received law unquote makes the contracting of a second marriage while the first one is still subsisting an offence . . . We call it bigamy . . . But Bemba society is polygamous and therefore bigamy is completely foreign to that society . . . It would be in the interest of justice in this case if the Court found that the accused never knew of the existence of bigamy . . . or if the Court conceded the possibility that, in spite of accused's apparent sophistication, this was so . . . I therefore ask the Court to find that the accused is entitled to the benefit of the doubt and to discharge him accordingly.

Let them do the worst — backward reactionary curators of British law in glass cages . . . You will send me to prison for sure, but that is a minor hurdle. I am destined for great things, you Che Chimimba, you English judge sitting there with your wig on in this tropical heat your asses frothing with authority . . . you'll eat your words one day . . . as for you Englishman, you're the last of a dying breed of settlers . . . but this fat creature you have educated, modelled in your image — him I'll deal with when you're hanging like a discarded tyre children swing on — back there in your miserable country that began to go bankrupt and de-

*cay long before it lost the empire . . . I'll flush these cobwebs you call
the Marriage Ordinance out of the system yet . . . you'll see . . . I'm destined for great things, you flea hunters.*

I came into the afternoon session when the public was allowed back
in — to hear the judgment. What a day, that fourth of April 1969!
There had been a slight drizzle at noon. Now the sun was out again. The
air was cooler, but the tightly-packed courtroom was full of body heat.
The judge's words were few. When he said, 'I have not the slightest hesi-
tation in finding him guilty as charged and he is so convicted,' the
people in the court seemed to breathe like one single animal. Asibweni
simply sat like a rock, staring in front of him, his face not moving. His
eyes sat deep in his head. Like that, he made me think of the baboon
captain who always sits high on a rock, looking out to the land below
for any enemies.

'Will the accused please rise . . .'

Twelve months in prison, the judge pronounced. No option of a fine.
Suddenly a shriek seemed to hit the roof, then the walls. Before I could
know where it came from mai wamung'ono Tirenje had reached the Prosecutor's seat banging hard on his desk and beating on her chest. On top
of this she was wailing, 'My man, bring back my man! . . . I want my
man! What do you all know about us? . . . If you had let me speak yesterday . . . I would have told you the whole story . . . how far we had
come together . . . He is guilty . . . he is guilty . . . The ancestors of Chirundu and Mirimba know it . . . but I did not bring up this case to give
you a football to play with . . . I wanted him to learn that I am the
right woman for him . . .' She turned to asibweni: 'Why do you not
come back Chimba? Chimbaaaaa! Has your tongue stuck to the roof of
your mouth? Has that woman really bewitched you — what have you
eaten of hers that has thrown this night between us? You are no longer
a government man, can you not listen to your own heart now you are
free? Chimbaaaaa — come baaaaack!'

Even as she was wailing, the police and the clerk of the court were
gently trying to calm her down and pull her away, out of the courtroom. I went to join her at the doorway. I took her away to her msuweni's house.

I could not leave her alone for the rest of the day. I had to wait for
her cousin to return from work. I had sent word to the Loco anyway to
tell them that I could not return to work for the afternoon. Almost two
of the three hours for which my pay would be cut were gone.

The happenings of the next three weeks were like nothing I had ever known. The terror of it shook me up so badly that I was left wondering what kind of animal we create when we shout and boo and dance and shriek and elect people and never get to know how government works, even while we are forming it, let alone afterwards. I wondered too about my own public life. I would have to get out. And yet again I felt I was being sucked into trade union work. Something seemed to hold me down in the movement. I felt as if I had been pushed out of a cocoon by these events. I seem to hear a voice tell me this was how I was meant to begin. Three years ago, early 1966 — and yet it seemed only yesterday that I was thrown into town life. Maybe asibweni Chimba was right when he warned me to keep out of this thing: it was too heavy for my tender years. And yet again I had been irritated by his warning. Maybe there is something in what that prison halfwit always shouts when he begins and ends an order with *Kwacha!* Because it is always a new day, it seems we are always having to wake up, as the slogan tells us to do: wake up, it's a bright new day! We seem to be always at the starting point, as I recall a Gambian poet says . . .

First we put off the strike of the transport workers for two weeks from the time asibweni was sent to jail after the trial. Just so that his acting successor might use the time to do better than reject our words outright. An idiot who didn't seem to know his left from his right, in spite of the assistance of his able Permanent Secretary. He tried to stall as long as possible, waiting for a donkey to give birth to a couple of piglets, maybe. So we decided on 19 April to lay down tools.

We did not have any funds that we could eat from if the government decided to keep us hanging long enough for us to starve. Our reorganized movement was only three years old. But we reckoned that if our wages were raised, and life made better in other ways, we could raise our union fees, even later invest in a co-operative store. We were prepared to gamble. The capital city had about twelve thousand males without work, out of a population of some 300 000. Fifty thousand males were roaming the provinces out there, looking for work. But drivers are not hatched overnight. We reckoned there couldn't be any scabs . . .

But the week after the trial the two Portuguese spies appeared before a magistrate. A little yellow African from Ghana, with a tough mind. He ordered them to go to jail for five years and fined them one thousand kwacha each. The city was full — full of happy noises. A month before, Portuguese planes had bombed two of our villages near the Zambesi. The people and the newspapers and the government saw this as a sign that the Portuguese were losing their sense, desperate because they were failing to rout the guerilla fighters in Angola.

Then, it seemed the sun was rising in the west, or the donkey had gone into labour with a couple of piglets. An English judge, who had primarily served in Singapore, threw out the magistrate's verdict and the penalty with it. Said the sentence had been too heavy, pointed out some mistake in the way the magistrate had looked at the facts, said the Portuguese might well have strayed across the Angolan border. Just as they claimed. The Chief Justice, an Irishman, agreed with the judge. They had no intention to spy. Ancestors alive! A member of the British parliament had visited the bombed villages after that earlier incident. Reported to his parliament that he did not think the Portuguese had intended to bomb the villages. Anyhow, he said, our people had made a few bombed houses seem like a city in ruins. Ancestors alive!

Those two wigs could not have picked a worse week to upset the people: the week of the strike. The Youth Brigade of the ruling party marched on the Court Building, led by the Commissioner for External Liberation movements. A crazy clown who always walked like a man trying to bring a herd of goats to order on a rainy day. The kind that nevertheless comes in useful for marches against foreign institutions. They mobbed the building. The Chief Justice had to make a run for it to hide in a nearby church house until dark.

Then there was mai wamung'ono Tirenje, who was seen among the Youth Brigade that night, and the strikers. During that week the night skies were one lurid blazing dome.

'Listen to me Moyo,' Tirenje's cousin said, 'I shall take my fourteen days' leave for the year earlier than I wanted to. It is not good that your mai wamung'ono should travel alone — she should not have come to the city alone for such heavy matters — I will go with her to Musoro. So she will stay here for two or three weeks longer while I talk with my employers about the leave. Will that be right?'

Yes, mai, it will be good. Tell me, do you think she will take him back if he makes up his mind to return during the year he will be out there?'

'She has told me that he has already made up his mind not to have her. She will leave matters in the hands of a lawyer here to arrange for them to cut the bond between them.'

'I understand, mai. Stay in peace.'

No, I could not run out of labour union work. Not now. It seems the events of my life were put together to carry me to this point. I don't know. It seems the fever has entered my mind. I see a hill ahead of me which I must climb to view what is beyond. No, shaken up though I was to be, the string of events that threw me into the life of the big city seem from this point to have been loaded with a significance many, many miles long.

I was a mere twenty-one when old grandfather Mutiso and I came to live in Kolomo Camp on the western edge of the capital. One of those shanty towns the British administration allowed to spring up, scrambled together by the scores of people who were sweeping down from the provinces, because the land could not hold them. The whites had taken most of the best land when England began to rule our country. We used to learn in primary school that only nine per cent of our country was fit for farming. The rest was poor soil, the tsetse fly made cattle farming impossible. If a man did not go to the copper mines, he had either to go and work for a white farmer or try to fight with the soil on his munda to yield food. The English were too busy governing us to bring us better ways of caring for the soil. The white people had come in large numbers from England and South Africa when the copper mines showed promise from 1920 onwards. More came here after 1940, we are told. But although the copper mines were bringing in money, nothing was done to use it to make it worthwhile for us to live on the land. Our people began to troop into the towns.

Our shanty town was meant to house people while they were waiting for town council houses to be built. But there were three shanty towns when we arrived. Houses stood in rows as if they were going to march like a bedraggled army any time. We had come from villages where the houses had been built first, then footpaths made their way in and out as best they could. We went to the open field to relieve ourselves. In Kolomo we had to go to small buildings with buckets in them. Our villages in Zembe have clean streets. The streets of Kolomo are full of holes, puddles, black mud, sick lean dogs, unfriendly people. Everybody seems to be in trouble . . .

I had written to an old schoolmate of mine in Kolomo to ask him to find us a shack we could buy. That was the only way you could find one. Then you paid rent to the City Council for the ground where the shack stood. Just then, he knew a young man who wanted to let his shack to someone while he was away. As he could often be away for a month or two at a time, he wanted a tenant who would not mind if he, the owner, wanted shelter for a night or two when he stopped in the city.

'Sell the cow, child of my son,' Old Mutiso said, 'you can buy the shanty if he wants to sell it one day. Go away from this place. Our ancestors lie here, but they will protect you on your journey. Soon they will be calling me to join them.' So Ambuye said. 'An old man can never be left alone to starve and die — others will look after these old bones and bundle them up for the grave when the time comes. You son of my son — son of Mutiso — shake off the dust of Zembe and carry on the name of our clan — there must be a better life for a young man like you — full of joy and fight like a young bull. Something new may be waiting for you to do and live for — me, I want to die here.'

This was at the end of 1965. Soon after we buried father.

'No, Ambuye,' I said, 'I do no such thing. The cow I will go and sell, but you come with me. We shall leave my sister with our aunt, and I shall come back for her when I have found a job and a decent dwelling.' Ambuye narrowed his small eyes — eyes that were a muddy brown — stared in front of him as if he were trying to listen to other voices.

'It is all right child of my son.'

We visited the Elephant, as the ruler of our Kazembe district is called, to pay our respects.

'You old rascal Mutiso you!' the Elephant said in his usual manner. 'At your age — going off as if you were chasing Ngoni warriors or running away from them — you must be thinking Chewa and Yao and Arabs are after you, eh?'

I was tickled but dared not laugh aloud. Beer was brought in.

'You always make fun of me, child of the son of Sibambo — but it is good to see the Elephant in good health — trumpeting with a glad heart. Greetings, Elephant!'

'Greetings, son of the child of Manaka — rascal you! Where do you think you are going — leaving us, are you? You think you will escape our droughts our floods our malaria — all our ills!'

The beer passed around among the three of us as we sat in the ample shade of the big tree.

'You and I have come a long way, Elephant — we have chased rabbits and buck and kudu and dassies and birds — all of them — we have known the cruelty of Ngoni the stupid pride of Chewa — not to talk of the slave-hounds — those Yao jackals and their Arab masters — we have together seen how far the leopard can spring how evil its claws — we both know the home of *sato*. Now the house of Mutiso has fallen . . .'

'Are you saying son of Manaka —'

'Do not leap into my mouth — if the house has to be raised it will have to be somewhere else — this is what is gnawing at my heart — my heart is heavy, dark clouds have fallen over my spirits — do you think I have not lain through nights with my eyes open waiting to hear what the ancestors have to say? Do you think my late son did not sacrifice goat after goat to ask the ancestors to lift the curse that has held down his house since the day when his cattle did that unspeakable thing?'

Grandfather's bitterness touched the Elephant. 'Who can know what the gods intend?' the big man said. 'Seriously now — the house of Mutiso has fallen yes — these are changing times — I need not tell you that — your grandson here will raise your house again — it will not matter where — you will still be in this land where your ancestors live — your grandson is not a man without a shadow — he has been to school he has hands — so your house still stands, Old Mutiso, to put it in other words — I do not speak to my councillors this way but to you I say sometimes my heart beats in a way that makes me tremble to think of the big things that have to be done — look at us Mutiso: we are a people that have travelled a road surrounded by disease drought and famine — so many things — our cattle goats and sheep have been eaten up by disease too — look at our homesteads: who is left who can boast a herd more than the fingers of one hand? We have no way of getting water during drought — we still think we can fight every animal disease by driving ticks into the dipping tank — no, we must have new ways of doing things — and yet do we also want to lose the wisdom of our ancestors? Should our youth no longer respect old age? I see these young upstarts from the towns when they have visited here or when the rulers like me have met them in the big city — I see them strut about like giraffe that see only the tree tops and not the part of the tree that is the beginning of life — or like billygoats that see only the female they want to ride and little beyond — tell me Mutiso should we stray away from the fountain simply because we are looking for new grazing? Yes indeed the grazing is tired and we are bound to look for other fields and yet I want to weep to see our young leaders — they act as though they understood all about the new grazing they have found — they go strutting about shouting *kwacha!* — yes it is indeed a new day and the sun is out and bright — we should wake up — but I have seen the very ones who shout *kwacha! wake up!* listen to white people telling them how to run their lives and those of the nation — what do you say Moyo?'

I looked down, rubbed my nose and then said, 'I do not know, my lord, my head is still mixed up, my lord.'

'I can see. Go well Mutiso my dearest friend may the gods keep you and your grandson — may they heal the pain in your hearts and help you raise the house of Mutiso again.'

I stood aside to let the two men speak to each other. 'Take this gift my friend,' the Elephant said, pulling a rug from under a stool, giving it to Ambuye. 'This is to use wherever you arrive. Let peace attend you when you sit and sleep on it.' His eyes were laughing when he added, 'You should long long ago have married again, Mutiso, after your last wife died — look at me: I am not much younger than you but I can still make any of my three wives scream and moan, ha-ha-ha!'

Grandfather laughed and laughed, his tongue whipping around in his mouth as if it wanted to be released but was at the same time unwilling.

'A new day, my old old friend — you are walking into a new day out there in the city. Do not let it blind you.'

'Elephant! Peace!' Ambuye shouted.

We took the long dusty road to the capital by bus.

A few days after we arrived in Kolomo Camp there was a big rally at Matero Stadium. We were told that the country was celebrating the second year of Independence. I went to the Stadium. The few times I had seen so many people in one place had been back home, when the Elephant had called the villages together to tell them about the harvesting or about Independence or about our dead heroes. There was also the time when the President had come to speak just before Independence — to ask the people to vote for him and his Party. But this day at Matero the crowd seemed to be mad with joy. The crowd frightened me a little. Their shouts and yells — *Kwacha! Kwacha! Kwacha!* — felt like a mighty wind that wanted to lift me from the ground and toss me over.

On my way back to Kolomo, in the bus, I read *Nation Times,* the evening paper. I could still hear the yells and shouts. The members of the Cabinet had been shifted from one job to another, the paper said. Asibweni — my uncle — had been made Minister of Transport and Public Works. I read aloud, 'Mr Chimba Chirundu has been Minister of Internal Affairs since Independence in 1964.' It said that the President might not have been pleased with Chirundu in Internal Affairs. The writer mentioned the event of March: the day Mrs Christine Muli, wife of Dr Muli, Minister of Education, was sent out of the country. Mr Chirundu had been forced to expel the lady. Then there were twelve African refugees in jail, locked up for being in the country without travel papers.

They had been ordered out but Chirundu refused to give them papers to travel. As they could not leave, the refugees were jailed — some from Zimbabwe, from South Africa, one from Mozambique, one from Angola.

The bus stopped and jerked forward and stopped and jerked. I got off at my station. Then I stood still against an electric pole. Just as if I really needed something to lean on. Because a news item in the paper held me. I was going to read it when a bus screeched to a stop. Before I could get myself together, I realized the passengers were singing: school children from the Stadium. Earlier in the afternoon I had seen them lining the streets in the burning sun, waiting for the President and the line of government cars to pass; sleek black cars following a Rolls Royce. Then the children looked as if they might wilt in the sun. Little did I realize that I was to see this pattern repeated again and again: children drilled to stand for hours in the sun waiting for the President's motorcade to pass . . . But there in the arena again the children stood with the crowds, many with their hands on their heads, listening to hours of speech broken into by music and dance, still under the shimmering Capricorn blaze. Now in the bus, they were full of life again, as if ready for another session of dance, music and speech.

I walked on to enter the township. I remembered the item I wanted to read and stopped. Page 3: WOMAN CAUGHT IN THE COILS OF PYTHON. The story sent a cold shiver through my veins, in spite of the warm if dry air around.

I found Ambuye Mutiso sitting against the front wall of the shack which faced west. The sun was tumbling down the western sky. 'Dusk is lasting shorter as one grows older,' he mumbled. 'Dusk used to be long when I was a boy back there in the old country in Malawi.'

'You are not going to eighty-three after eighty-four Ambuye,' I said. He stretched out his legs, straightened his back against the wall, making gurgling sounds in the mouth: 'Ah, now the blood is running free again.' Then he folded his knees again, rested the sinewy back of his left hand on one knee. With the right he tipped his snuff out of a small tin onto the dark left palm. He pushed the tin between two fingers of the left hand, cupped the snuff in that hand, took a pinch with the pointing finger and thumb of his right hand. When he pulled the powder into one nostril after the other, Ambuye was a picture of perfect peace. He then rubbed his nose with two strokes of the back of his hand and his eyes were filled with water. 'Aaaah,' he exhaled. 'I have just been thinking you should be home.'

'Moni, Ambuye!'

'Moni, my son!'

'Mulibwanji?'

'Zikomo ndilibwino. How was the day?'

'Wooooooo, the number of people, Ambuye! You should have been there.'

He was tickled. When he laughed only one brown tooth showed in the bottom gums and two in the top row. The tongue skipped around as if any moment it was going to push the teeth over without any effort.

'Something terrible happened this morning, Grandpa.'

He grunted, listening.

'A woman was nearly killed by a python. In fact they say she may die — the paper says she is lying ill in her village.'

'*Sato, sato,*' Old Mutiso mumbled, nodding his head a few times, looking straight into the wall of the opposite shack, about six paces away.

'Yes, *sato,* Ambuye. Two women were gathering wood in the bush and the snake coiled itself around one. Two men who were walking in the bush heard her moan. They rushed to where she was. They beat and slashed and stabbed the reptile with their pangas and sticks. The python loosened its hold. It threshed about and slid away into the thicket, bleeding. The other woman simply fainted.'

'*Sato, sato,*' Ambuye kept mumbling, still looking at the blank wall. 'You know, *sato* does not often want to kill a person. The gods who sent him must have a reason. Like that, even if he dies in that bush or on the rocks, you will never find him again.'

Ambuye's voice trembled. 'I have not seen *sato* in years,' he said, almost in a mumble — 'I always longed to see him again before I die — but you cannot just go out to hunt for him — he has to appear before you — those who hunt him can only be up to mischief.'

'You wish you had been there, Ambuye, where the woman was attacked?'

'Yes, child of my son.'

'Oh wake up old man,' I teased, 'your days of the python are over — but do not get any ideas about leaving us.'

'You are not my prisoner, I am not yours.'

I laughed, thinking *but we are, we are prisoners but it does not matter.*

'You like to tease me, child of my son, to laugh — that is good. I know you have already met *sato*. Everyone needs to know him — he is king, ancestor — you need to look at him a long time even though you are frightened — everyone has something he fears most — so much, his fart could kill a tribe of crocodiles — but when you have come face to face with the thing you dread most, or peep into its sleeping place and see it, that fear will make you strong -- to know the size of *sato* is to know the size of your fear the size of your liver the size of the stone you need to swallow for the strength you need.'

I remembered then part of the news story that told how the woman in the python's coils had taken off her headkerchief with her free arm and covered the snake's head.

Old Mutiso spat in front of him, pulled the mucus through the nose and throat and spat again. He scratched himself in the armpit, nodding his head all the time. 'When a god has got you in his coils,' he said, 'it is folly to look at him.'

'I will make us some food, Ambuye.'

I had seen *sato* — the python — when I was about ten. It was near the white man's farm. I was with a few other children whose parents were farm labourers. We ran to tell the white farmer, but not before we had stood for a few moments, staring at the creature, I with my heart in my throat. The white man came and shot it. The older people told what sorrow would follow because of the killing. But they also said there had once been a mean python in the same bush. It had not always been mean to people, they said. White hunters had been combing the bush for *sato* so that they could take the skin or take him alive in a cage.

When we saw *sato*, my sister and I were spending our school holidays with our parents who were working for the white farmer. During the school months we lived with Ambuye in Kazembe, where my parents had come from in the beginning.

I am easily tickled and laugh aloud easily. I liked to play jokes on people when I was younger. Anything for a good laugh. I did not care if others were not amused. But the appearance of *sato* was no laughing matter.

As we sat on the floor eating Ambuye said, as if he were summing up something we had been talking about, 'Do not marry late, like your late father did — it is foolish and wasteful.'

I laughed and laughed. 'I am no fly that is easily going to drop into a cup of milk,' I replied, 'this is a city and a number of friends who came here five or six years ago have spread ugly stories at Kazembe about the ways of town girls.' I could not tell Ambuye the big scare these stories caused among my age group back home. And I swore to myself to move with great care. When a man came back with a venereal disease our people said he had been bitten by a woman. Horrible pictures formed in our minds as teenagers. We had wild fancies of how when you are in there, without the girl knowing it even, her thing could close you in, suck on your penis and when there was nothing left to suck, bite you painfully on the tip. Then the girl's thing would release you and you would go wandering sick with swollen balls and shrinking penis. Oh the terror of it! We believed the girls in Kazembe were clean and could not bite.

'You cunning rabbit you!' Ambuye remarked. 'It is this story about *sato,*' he continued, his eyes glistening in the dim light of the paraffin lamp, 'that reminds me about your late father, and that always takes my mind back to that terrible day — I have told you many times before — it shows how one thing goes into another and this also goes into another and you see how the ancestors work through the animals and the trees and the rivers — you feel the mystery of things child of my son.'

'Tell it me again Ambuye.'

The old man's mind wandered freely back to those early days. The days when Tumbuka people were spilling over the north-eastern border from Nyasaland. Because Tumbuka had been sat on for so long by Ngoni, Chewa, Bemba in their own country, one after another. I reckoned that my father, Mutiso, the last of Ambuye's seven children, must have been about thirty-three when his people came to settle in the Kazembe area near the border. One day, Ambuye told, as if from nowhere, the sun right overhead, three cows came thundering through the village and charged into my father's homestead — moving with a most unearthly noise, running this way and that while they dragged their hooves and dug and scraped the surface of the yard and pushed one another until the surrounding walls fell — their udders swung and beat about — then they made for the door of my father's hut, jostling to be first through the entrance — stamped about inside and brought the walls down — your mother snatched you away and ran into another hut — what an evil omen, how evil — everybody said it — a thing we had never — never — seen.'

Then came the drought. The worst in the north-eastern district in years. Maybe the cows had been frightened by a python, people said . . . or some other unfriendly animal . . . Why should they choose Mutiso's house instead of taking to savanna land? . . . evil spirits perhaps . . .

must be. Tumbuka of Kazembe district have known many periods of drought. The direction of the wind, the feel of the clouds, will tell them when the coils of drought are gathering around the land. Old men and women will look to all the cardinal points, trying to read the signs. When they shake or nod their heads and when you see their craggy faces, you sense how deep is their knowledge, their understanding — after generations of life in this area. Yes, we have known years of plenty, of well-being. When drought sets in, we get ready in our minds for the cycle that must be. Always there is no way out. We must depend on what other people can give or sell. Meantime the land lies like a bedridden woman, shrivelling up, wasting away unable to help herself, taking nothing, yielding nothing and yet unable to go into the grave. All we do is look at her, shake our heads and despair. The earth cakes, trees prefer to lose their leaves because there is only enough to feed the stem and the branches. Wild game wander away from their territory, move up and down the Luangwa valley to get what they can. The tortoise seems to be the only creature that knows the secret of the drought. The hawk stays longer on the wing because its would-be prey is much more restless ... And so the drought holds us tighter in its coils, dumb and unfeeling like *sato*, like a god. If *sato* has had his meal before the drought the eleven to twelve months he lies there without any need for food may just carry him through.

The Elephant always had the wisdom to tax the people. At each harvest every family is taxed a bag of sorghum or maize which goes into one of the communal silos. In drought the old and sickly people and others who cannot work or hunt for themselves eat from this store together with the rest. Not to lean too much on the store, able-bodied young men go out to seek work on white people's farms along the rail zone where the best land is, where whites know how to save water — land that stretches twenty miles to the east and twenty miles to the west of the line. Or they go to the towns, including the copper mine.

A kind of diarrhoea swept my youngest sister into the grave. My mother stopped having children. We had also the tsetse fly which killed off cattle ...

So it was that my father had to go to the line of rail in the west to work on maize and dairy farms. We — father, mother and the remaining sister — went to live in Bisa.

'Your father was cleansed by the doctor,' Old Mutiso often told me, 'and yet nothing ever came right.'

'Those who want to go seek work elsewhere,' the Elephant ruled at the time, 'may go. But they must not leave the land untended, it is a gift from the ancestors. Already the mines at Kalate have swallowed many of our young men. On each plot of ground there must be at least one able-bodied man who can try to wake it up from this deep sleep when the rains come. For rain must come. A piece of land with no one to till it will be given to any one of my people who needs it. Remember we have still many of our Tumbuku across the border where the sun rises. If they come to me and want to live here I cannot deny them land and I do not care if the British government across the seas drew the line that divides us.'

This Ambuye often recited to me and I grew up with the knowledge from his lips. He would not be expected to know that six thousand years ago early man made simple stone tools in this Central African country; that around 8000 B.C. the San roamed the country, making hunting weapons, listening to the voices of their own ancestors. They left rock paintings in Kazembe — long before they drifted south. Old Mutiso, now eighty-four, would perhaps have grown up listening to Tumbuka songs that told of the people who took the place of the San two thousand years ago. People who came from the north, bringing with them the ways of making iron tools out of stone and of making earthen pots. What he spoke with certainty was the history of Tumbuka since the Bantu-speaking Africans swept down from the north two hundred years later. This land was already being tilled when the new strangers came with their cattle. He knew from our songs and stories about the kingdoms that rose and crumbled . . .

The Elephant's knowledge of history also goes back to that point. The people's epic poetry still talks about the great migrations of three hundred years — beginning from about the sixteenth century. 'Our elders of long ago,' I heard him often remind the people at great gatherings, such as the one he called on the event of that fierce drought, 'do not forget what our elders tell us . . .' At this point the poet of the people stood up and came forward toward the Elephant's stool. He was grey-haired and had a drooping lower jaw. He waved his fly-swish and looked first at his lord, then at the people, turning his body full circle at the same time. Like one who wanted to make it clear that there could be no competition in his job. Then in a high-pitched voice he recited his tale: the migrations from the Congo basin where the Luba Kingdom thrived . . . how the peoples who went east until they hit Lake Malawi built the kingdom of Maravi . . . a kingdom made up of Nyanja, Chewa and Nsenga . . . those far-off days when all the country

around Shire River teemed with Nyanja . . . how Chewa, led by fierce
kings like Undi and Mwase enslaved Tumbuka in the Luangwa basin —
the very ancient ancestors of the people he was singing for . . .

'But we Tumbuka of the hills,' the old poet went on, 'and our Tonga
friends of the lake came from where the sun rises to live in the same
land with Maravi — we were never a war-loving people — this was why
every hyena thought he could bite a fat piece of meat from our body —
that is why every hawk thought he could dive down on any chicken in
our midst and make away with it — we are not cowards like the man
who with his fart keeps off a tribe of crocodiles that are still a number
of strokes away from the canoe — and no Tumbuka can be someone's
fool — Tumbuka are like the animal that goes underground and comes
out at the other end — Mwase and Undi were not the only ones who
thought to urinate into the mouths of Tumbuka — only yesterday this
most recent yesterday Ngoni came and gave Tumbuka and Tonga a time
of fire and terror — only yesterday this most recent yesterday the
hounds they call Yao gave Tumbuka and Tonga years of terror — the
hounds stole the people by night to sell to the Arabs as slaves . . .'

Thus the poet explained as always how it was that many Tumbuka
and Tonga fled further north and west. Here they found peace for a
while. Then the white rulers had come and cut a line through the land
so that the part to the east would be Nyasaland — a line that split Tumbuka in two. 'But it did not end here my fellow men — Tumbuka had
found other groups that had broken away from the kingdom of Luba —
the kingdom of Mwata Yamvo. We found Lunda under the great king
Kazembe, Bisa and Bemba under their king Chitimukulu — people who
were here a long long time . . .'

Historians tell us that Lunda, Bisa and Bemba had been settled here
since the sixteenth century. But the closest neighbours of Tumbuka
were Bemba, who occupied mostly the western Luangwa valley. The
great Kazembe had settled his people much farther west. In the middle
of the nineteenth century, we are told, when the later waves of Tumbuka were fleeing from the fire of Ngoni warriors and Yao slave hounds
and spilling into upper Luangwa, Bemba and Lunda were still the most
powerful people of Luba blood.

'Chitimukulu of Bemba,' the Tumbuka poet said, 'also tried to
throw us into the teeth of Luangwa's crocodiles — because they thought
Tumbuka were farting cowards — but Tumbuka's head was quicker
than his spear . . .'

'Today,' the Elephant summed up, 'Tumbuka, Nyanja, Bemba,

Lunda live together in this part of the country — under the law the white man brought — we are all the same — no one can come and foul up our houses.'

'The white man's ways,' Ambuye would often say, 'favour the strong — the strong in money, learning and numbers. Even though the white man's law put us together, the white man favours the strong over the weaker, he gives the strong more power.'

But for the moment the matter most urgent was this drought. We raised our hands to hood the eyes, looked far into the distant blue. All we saw were specks of cloud. 'We never could understand the workings of the spirits in times like these,' Old Mutiso would remark. 'You had merely to wait and try to see it through because you knew that there is nothing that never comes to an end.'

'Go now, my children,' the Elephant said, 'Let us go and settle matters with our family ancestors. They will provide for their children.'

And the people felt strong enough again to face the coming days. The words of the poet lifted their spirits. If we had lived beyond the spear and fire of Ngoni, Chewa, Bemba, Yao slave hounds, the white man's government, beyond some of the diseases that surrounded us, we could outlive the drought. I was to learn when I was older that we shall have to learn to do more than merely outlive calamity.

My father had to send me and my sister back to Kazembe for schooling. His younger brother had stayed behind with Old Mutiso, we would live with them. The schools in Bisa were only for the children of white farmers. He and my mother worked and worked. Each new day my mother, even more than my father, seemed to be growing thinner, weaker. They always hoped that they would save enough money for them to be able to return to Kazembe and raise the fallen walls of our homestead, give life to our munda again. After five years on the white man's farm they could not put off their return any longer. My uncle left for the mines at Kalate to try his luck there. 'Your brother was not made to be a farmer,' Grandfather Mutiso told my father.

Back in Kazembe life went from bad to worse. Something inside my father seemed to have simply broken down. I could not understand it. I had always known him as a strong man — strong as a steel plough. He worked much harder than his younger brother. I remembered that I had begun to see the change even before we left for Bisa. He seemed not to be with us anymore. Now it all comes back in my memory, it seemed that he had found a road and taken it, but the road led away from us.

He was not interested in the munda any longer. I could not feel him anymore. He spent much time in the village across the stream, drinking. The only time he brightened up and talked freely to us was when he was drunk. Whenever he told my mother he was going to the village across the stream he said, 'Woman, we are going to chain the lunatic.' I found out this was a kind of club expression for drinking beer. It made me sad to know I could not feel my father any more. He was not even rough with my mother or his children, as some men become when they live on strong corn beer. He did not use bad language or rave like a caged animal. He was always gentle with us, but he was going down. One season we had food, another season we lived on charity or my mother grew pumpkin which she bartered for sorghum or maize.

'You must go for another cleansing,' Ambuye Mutiso advised. 'We must keep talking to the ancestors.'

Father was not unwilling. Those were the days Ambuye used to tell me the full story for the first time: the event of the cows that came thundering and mooing into our homestead.

'You know too my daughter,' I would hear Ambuye say to mother, 'he has never been the same man since that dark cloud fell over us.'

Just after I had been circumcised, father went for a cleansing.

There was no change.

My mother was beginning to drag her feet around the homestead. She told me, 'Moyo, I cannot even bend down to pick up a pot of water at the river or put it down from my head.' And to my sister she said, 'My little aunt, you are going to do more things in this house than before, you are going to be a woman even before you are ready for it.'

She died. My uncle Chimba came from the city for the funeral. He took care of everything as there was no money in the house. My other ambuye, Chimba's father, also came from Shimoni. He did not look like my own blood grandfather, my own mother's father — the way he carried himself for the two days he was with us. He was sulky, did not seem to have a sense of fun. He was a total stranger, like a man who happened to stop by to see us. I knew the story of how he had thrown out my grandmother. My mother and Chimba had been very fond of each other. We had gone to the burial of his first child. Ambuye Mutiso used to say that their attachment was because they had not sucked from the same mother. Then I saw him again when politicians were coming through Kazembe to ask the people to take out the Party card. He looked very important, full of spirit. I got to know later that he had spoken to my father about his ways but found he simply could not reach him.

Nine months later, in September of 1965 my father died.

'The last of the fences is down, child of my son,' Grandfather said to me, 'so now the ancestors have told us the truth at last.'

'How come you are still kicking about, Ambuye?' I teased.

'Oh be off with you madcap!'

Grandfather Mutiso was born in the dark times of *chifwamba* — the Arab and Yao slave raids in Nyasaland. Which could have been about 1884. 'When I was only that small,' he would say, 'my father and mother — my father whose name you have taken — my parents were always running away to some place — in the dark they carried me on their backs or towed me by the hand because people reported that Yao were in the village — those Yao dogs were not like anybody else in the land — they were not like Tonga, not like Nyanja nor Nsenga — they came from the south and were yellow in the face — they broke doors and took young men and women to sell to the Arabs — I remember one cousin of mine came back after many moons — he ran away after the Arabs had taken them across the water — he said he heard tell that the slaves were taken to the sea to be sold again — so much was happening those days my son — you should have been there to hear my father tell of the proud fierce Ngoni who came from the land of Zulu under Zwangendaba — you should have been there to see men like Joni Chilembwe — I met him when I was on my way to join the army for the big war against the Germans — I was a young man when Chilembwe led his people against the white man — he was Christian and said his church was going to save the people from the rule of the white man . . .'

Later when I looked up history books in the big city to find out more about the things Ambuye had told me, I came to think of him with deeper awe. There was my own grandfather, I thought, my own blood, who had brought a history of turmoil with him into the heady days of *kwacha* and independence — and yet these days passed him by, simply passed him by as you do a person you do not know. Indeed men like him, like the Elephant, would not be known in the deeper sense of the word, in the full recognition of children of a great history. And as I dug into history and thought about it for my nightschool studies, I wondered all the more that Malawi should have become the saddle for the kind of man its President is: a medical doctor who had lived so long abroad that history had also passed him by, but for other reasons. Ambuye and the Elephant are history, and the young politicians are leaping over them; like when you constantly jump over a sick person in a crowded house, because you would not have it said that you hastened his death. Here is a country — Malawi — that was the crossroads of so much history. Before Chilembwe's brief revolt in 1915 which led to his death, there were the Scottish mission stations; there was Zwangendaba who had fled north from Shaka of Zulu, his conquest of Tumbuka of the north-western hills, and of Tonga of the western lake shore, his death further north in 1845. There were the attempts in 1875 of Tumbuka and Tonga kingdoms to rise against their Ngoni lords. After that first time when Ngoni was helped by Chewa — Mwase's kingdom in the west — Tumbuka realized what they were up against. Ngoni proved this another time when they speared to death hundreds of Tumbuka and Tonga survivors on the Hora mountains.

When Harry Johnston — 'Jonisoni' — became the first British Commissioner and Consul General in 1891, the Arab and Yao slave trade began to slow down. They hated the Britisher for it. But at the same time more whites entered the country to settle. The king of Maravi saw the land slip from under his people's feet when the whites began to make deals with the English rulers. It became the fate of Ambuye to keep running. If you were not taken into slavery, the white planter could lure you to his plantation; or else someone from the gold mines in the south trapped you into joining the workers who were willing to go with him.

'The white Christians were busy chewing off your backside,' Grandfather would say, 'while you were not looking and then you were ripe to be drawn into the mission station to work on church land — but you see my child — every one used to say Tumbuka stay in the cold river rather than come on to dry land to fight, but we stay alive longer and there at the end of the field you will see a Tumbuka shoot out of a hole . . .'

In spite of the trials of Tumbuka, the poet of the people recited with great zest their spirit of oneness. One thing the poet could be two-minded about was the arrival of Mlowoka. A wandering hunter and trader in ivory, he had simply arrived and, tired of his job, set himself up as king of Tumbuka near Lake Nyasa in the old country. He gave himself the title Chikulamayembe, marking the Kamanga dynasty that was to continue through the middle of the eighteenth century. An ordinary elephant hunter: there lay some of Tumbuka's shame in the beginning. But they were later to thank Mlowoka because he gave them back their pride. It was during the dynasty of Chikulamayembe that Tumbuka rose against Ngoni and Chewa. He was killed.

Because he had hunted elephant, the ruler of Zembe had taken the title Elephant. Which is also how the big school the people had built for themselves and with their own hands was called Kamanga Community School. In all his wanderings the Elephant had learned the importance of a school education. The people simply got up and built it. The colonial administration in the city registered it in 1939.

'One of these days you are going to laugh into the face of the sun and it will strike you blind,' my father often warned me. Because I laughed easily. I liked to hear the sound of my laugh. If I got into trouble because of it, my sister would come taunting me: 'I told you you would fall into the ditch laughing into the sky like that — I told you — I told you!'

'Go fart among the chickens!' I would say, trying to beat down the pain and keep from crying after a whacking from my father. I was always one for a good hearty guffaw. I laughed when I met wayside cripples, helped them but laughed to see how different they looked from other people. Why would they want to be different like that? I wondered. I would stand in the middle of the homestead, when I was eight, wait until some people were near, and fart like a donkey when it kicks the air around it with joy, head down, backside up. It made them curse and promise to chop my head off. I tried teasing Ambuye too. He would simply take his snuff and pretend to ignore me. A little later I would pass near him absent-mindedly, and before I knew it, his paw would be upon me. He had a strong grip, the old man. With the other hand he would pinch me between the thighs until I yelled for help. The deep brown marks on my thighs I earned bothered me only for a few moments, even while my eyes were still full of tears. After that, I would be planning another thing that used to make me laugh. There was a weed with thick, grey, furry leaves that we used to sneak up a boy's shorts, along his thighs, when he was having a nap out in the open. The stinging itch started him scratching, he sprang up bawling like a baboon, and hopped all over the place while we lay flat on our backs laughing. The more he scratched the more he was rubbing the juice of the leaves into his skin. The result was big lumps on his testicles and thighs. I did that to the village idiot. That afternoon I nearly saw my last sunset. He followed me to my home, bent on murdering me. Once we laughed at an old man who was walking to the bush to relieve himself. He must have made me out easily because I have a loud laugh. It was perhaps also more irritating than that of the other boys. For both these adventures I paid dearly under my father's swish. 'Repeat after me,' he ordered as the swish came down on my body, 'repeat: *I must always respect grownups, I promise never to laugh at an old man or a cripple!*'

There was another time when my father almost came down on me with two feet. A regular visitor and friend of the family had the habit of breaking the news of someone's death with a sentence we would use in Tumbuka if we wanted to say a river or well has dried out, 'the water has evaporated'. He would never say it with the grave tone in which grown-ups say 'passed away' or 'left us'. When he said it I would run out in order to laugh outside. The idea of it — a man drying out, evaporating, keeping quiet for good, just drying out like that — that was just too comical. And our friend's face and voice made me feel all the more how silly and ridiculous it must be for a man to evaporate like that, fizzle out, perhaps without even telling anybody. But one day I exploded before I could stand up to run outside. I shut my mouth at once to choke off the laugh. Food particles and saliva spluttered and sprayed the space in front of me. 'When a person dies,' my father said as he belted me, 'it is no laughing matter you hear me!'

I found myself drawing closer and closer to Grandfather Mutiso as I grew up. He was always saying to me, 'Now do not tell anyone about this, it is our secret we two. . .'

When I was fourteen, my father said, 'Now listen Moyo, you are too big for a belting — but just remember this — the next time you are beaten it will be by the elders of our district and I hope that day will never come.' And thereafter it seemed my father did not care what I did since he could no longer beat me. I could not be sure. Only my mother continued to throw words with thorns at me if I did something stupid. Later, he did not talk to me much unless he was drunk. He was not interested in my schooling either. And Grandfather and I spoke more to each other; I asked him many, many questions about the history of our people. Although I told him a lot about what I was learning in school, he simply nodded and I knew he did not understand me. He often seemed to know just what I was thinking without my telling him. I tried to guess what *he* was thinking, but it was impossible. More and more I came to know that we did not have to ask each other, we just felt each other . . .

'You know what, child of my son,' Ambuye said when I was fourteen, 'Tumbuka pride was so high at one time that even Ngoni could not teach us their ways — like circumcision — but they married some of our women and Bemba and Tumbuka also mixed a little — so today we do circumcise boys your age.'

So it was I was circumcised.

In school I was not bright at all. I was not a duffer either. From grade to grade teachers kept saying, 'If only Moyo did not take school for a sportsground and play the fool so much . . .' In Grade Five I found a teacher who was famous for being able to 'skin you alive' if you crossed his path. I knew my laughs and guffaws would get me into trouble with him. How that man's cane could sting! He also liked to say, 'You will eat grass my boy!'

'Go to my house and ask my wife to give you my lunch,' he ordered me one day. 'I left too early this morning for her to make it.'

'Yes Teacher.'

'Go tell your teacher to go eat dung!' the teacher's wife said to me.

I puzzled over the woman on my way back. How could any woman say a thing like that to a man — her own man!

'How can a woman say such a thing!' a classmate said when we met on the road.

'If she wants to say that to her husband, why choose *me* to carry the message? How can I put it to Teacher?'

'Say his woman is not in.'

'He won't believe it. Or if she's still angry with him this afternoon she'll say, didn't the boy you sent tell you what I said? — I said tell your teacher to go eat dung! You know how women like to remind you exactly what they told you before just to use it against you.'

'Or maybe if you tell Teacher what she said and they are friends again this afternoon — all she needs to answer is *What boy? I never saw such a boy this morning.* And you know what? —'

'I'm going to skin you alive.' The picture of me standing there before Teacher, helpless, opened that valve inside me and I burst out laughing.

'Yes — go on laughing — it may be your last chance.'

If I was going to be punished, I thought, it should be for something concrete I'd done.

'Get out of my office, you'll pay for this with your hide — you'll eat grass!' So Teacher fumed when I reported.

Out there, I laughed and slid down against the wall facing the sun. I thought of Teacher's frayed collar, twisted, crumpled tie, patched jacket elbows and laughed at the idea of dung.

The next day he called me to the classroom.

'What my wife said to you yesterday — I want you to forget it, understand?'

'Yes Teacher.'

'That's all.'

'Yes Teacher.'

I suspected that he was bribing me not to tell the other pupils — and have it known in the school that he and his wife were fighting. I laughed and guffawed in class after this but he never punished me. He was always *going* to skin me alive and make me eat grass. He knew I knew that he knew . . .

'One of these days,' my mother said once, 'you will find yourself laughing right into the face of a python. I want to see what you do that day.' The idea itself sounded like a joke, until I saw *sato* with my own eyes at Bisa, where my parents were working for a white farmer. We had visited them during a school vacation, my sister and I. In a thicket near a river. He lay coiled up there as if nobody were nearby. It frightened me later to think that we might have stumbled right into his home had we not heard a deep and weird sound around us. We peered through the trees and there he was. A giant. We just knew it must be *sato*. I felt as if I had been glued to the ground, as if I could not shut my eyes to avoid this terrible sight. When we left the bush, it was to run and yell as I had never done before.

'*Sato!*' my mother gasped. We knew where not to stray after that day.

'You're always trying to clown and make other people laugh,' a school captain said to me, leading me to the principal for bad behaviour. 'In class, at assembly, on the playgrounds — you know, you're a pest.'

'You're wrong,' I said. 'I'm not trying to make anyone laugh. As long as a thing makes *me* laugh I don't care about other people. I'm not asking them to join me — I find a thing funny and I laugh — whether other people laugh with me or not — I'm amusing myself, not other people — I'm no clown either — don't you understand?'

He looked straight ahead of him, thinking, I could feel, that he was all the more right to take me in — so many boys and so many girls talked of me as crazy, while they laughed.

'Must one always have a good reason for laughing?' I asked the captain another time.

'Of course yes — otherwise you must be mad and must be sent to Chaivasha in the big city.'

'What should I not laugh at, tell me?'

'Dead people, dying people, dangerous people, crippled people, blind and deaf and dumb people, criminals.'

'*You're* mad, you must be mad, captain!'

'I hear you laugh at all these people.'

'Have you ever seen Sophie on the playground?'

'Yes — what of him?'

'Is he funny — does he make you laugh?'

'Of course yes.'

'He doesn't tickle *me*.'

'Everybody thinks he is funny — wanting us to play that game here — where have you ever seen boys play basketball — he must be a girl underneath. That's obvious.'

'He may be, but what's there to make you laugh? See — there can't be any rules — why do you want to think before you can laugh?'

Sophie was our nickname for one of the staff who told us he had learned basketball from an American lecturer when he was training as a teacher. One of the things that got under my skin was Sophie's attempts at being funny. 'How many Moyos make a Moyo-Moyo?' he often said when he saw me near him, and then chuckled. A donkey might have had more and better reasons for braying.

When Kamanga School feasted for its twentieth year, I was finishing Primary. The Secondary division had been set up five years before. So I simply went into Grade Eight, the beginning of high school.

Over the years, the school had sent out its own pupils for teacher training. When the secondary school started, the primary school teachers were sent out to the capital for up-grading. They returned to man the higher division.

The churches around pestered the Elephant and his councillors to allow them to come and teach Religious Knowledge. The people would not have it. We the pupils did not really understand these things, but even so we realized that two opposing camps were forming among our teachers. Today I can see better the forces that were at work. The teachers had come from missionary training institutions where they had to study Religious Knowledge as taught by a specific church. Some of the teachers had even come back converted to Christianity. One of the Elephant's trusted men was chairman of the school board. On behalf of our ruler, he made it plain that there was to be no competition between the churches for our souls.

One African travelling evangelist arrived in Zembe one day. He kept telling people he had seen Jesus Christ in a dream. As far as we knew, he was not of any particular church. At last he simply paced the dirt roads up and down, his mind clearly upside down. Either the people had already been captured by the churches around our district, or they were unwilling. The Elephant did not stop any of the missionaries coming and going as they liked; as long as they did not touch the school.

We got to hear from our teachers that the Education Department in the capital was pressing the Elephant to bring in 'Religious Knowledge' at Kamanga. They would withdraw their money for teachers' salaries if the school continued to be stubborn. The Elephant stood firm. The headmasters of both divisions argued that as 'Religious Knowledge' was not compulsory but only a possible in the list of subjects, they were teaching physiology instead. This kept the Education people quiet for a while.

When Kamanga was feasting for its twentieth year the chief speaker — an official from the capital — tried to urge us to bring in Religious Knowledge, even as an option. The Elephant, for his part, stood up and said that the British were a funny people — they reduced the African king to what they called *chief* — was it because England had a king and they could not bear to have black kings whom the people respected and honoured — he had told those white people in the capital that they should address him as 'Elephant' when they wrote to him, not 'Chief'. Now they wanted to teach us their god as if we did not have any. 'I have not heard of any of us going to white people to teach them about our gods, so why should they plague and divide our minds so? Our ancestors tell us that our gods are enough — the matter is finished.'

Of course the matter could never be finished. The Elephant was to realize this two years later. This was when the country was restless and excited and politicians went up and down the country to tell us that the time had long passed when we should be ruled any longer by Britain. Men came from the capital to whip up feeling all over. The Elephant welcomed them. He spoke praises to them, told them he would rather serve under an African government than white rulers. 'But one thing pains my heart,' the Elephant said, 'you young men are using the white man's holy scriptures to strengthen your words against white rulers — why? Can we not be free simply because human beings must be free — as we were long, long before the Christians came?'

I doubt, now I think back on it, if the Elephant could even have guessed what was to come. As the country neared self-rule, and soon after that big event, a Christian teacher from Kamanga was becoming a big name in politics. He gained a seat in parliament as a member for Kazembe district. With the help of the President, himself a Christian, the member for Kazembe was to use his political position to force Kamanga to accept Religious Knowledge into the system. The Elephant's councillors were to write many letters to the President to appeal against it and to try to keep the school free of this thing. Letters would simply be passed on to the Department of Education for their attention. The white officer, still a long way from being pensioned or paid out, would simply tear up the letters and throw the pieces into the wastepaper basket, maybe with a smile of contempt. He might rest his arm on the desk, light a cigarette and shout, 'Mabangi! would you make me some tea there please!' There were a number of reports of white officers like this one — officers who were happy when African ignored or snubbed or attacked African, because they would keep their jobs so much longer. I was to hear a lot from asibweni Chimba about those early days of fighting talk. That was before we clashed on the trade union's activities. He had got to know about the Elephant's appeals. Asibweni said to me then, 'The Englishman has perfected the art of containing conflict, mupwa. I'm sure those officers in Education must simply have said, "All that Elephant nonsense — that will stop — he'll get to know he's only a chief, damn it." Now tell me — when coon swallows coon what's an Englishman of good breeding to do but stand aside and take note? I sympathized with the Elephant very much those days, believe me mupwa. Today, I don't know.'

The political events of the three years following that school anniversary shook the country. Rulers like the Elephant must have wondered what they were being told to vote for. Two other teachers at Kamanga left, to go into politics. Other teachers left for other districts. Maybe they were also unsure of their future. Others again were to leave for government jobs which paid much better — for a life amid city lights and other attractions. Indeed, when I began secondary school, I realized things would never be the same again . . .

My own uncle Chimba was to leave school work for politics, wasn't he? I was too little and too blind to know that he would have it in him to become a politician, a very important man, when my mother took me and my sister to Kapiri to visit him. That was when he taught at the Seventh Day Adventist school. 'I am so proud to have a fine big nephew and a big beautiful niece,' he often said when he met us. When he married in 1959 at Musoro, we visited them, all four of us. Mai wamung-'ono, Tirenje, had a lovely round face, strong-looking shoulders and legs. She walked with the stride of a woman who knows where she is going to and at just what point she is going to stop and when she will return or change her course. I think I shall always remember her as I saw her those days. Also as I saw her at Kapiri in the early days of their life together. What is more, she took a liking to me at once. I remember it was in 1959-1960 when things were boiling furiously, people were being jailed, that my uncle's name was common talk in Zembe. We read his fiery speeches in the paper. He was mostly active in the Copperbelt.

I stayed in Secondary for three years, beginning in 1960. Because I could see that our house was falling, I left and took a job as an office clerk at my school in order to support the family and try to save money so that I could return to finish the last two years. It was not to be. My mother died. And then my father, in 1965. Did Ambuye Mutiso really know what the truth was the ancestors had been trying to tell the Mutiso house? Maybe. For me, I sensed it was the end of a chapter. Even before, Ambuye had said to me, 'Shake off the dust of Zembe and carry on the name of our clan . . .' The story of our people — who they are, where they came from — filled my mind with names of heroes and scoundrels, pictures of what they did and what they failed to do. I pictured what it would have been to live in those days of raids and wars, victory and flight, and I felt awed: I would not have had the liver to survive, and yet it would have been glorious to live through those days. Much closer to me had been famine disease, failure, collapse, death. Overnight it seemed that even the courage and bright hopes of the Elephant, of Kamanga Community School, were paltry. Things were mixed up in my head, I was unsure of myself, and angry with myself for it. Which was also why I decided to take Ambuye with me, apart from the plain fact that I felt his need of me — felt it like the very air one breathes. Also, perhaps through him I would be able to see some of the truths the ancestors wanted to reveal to me about myself and my rôle among other men . . .

My sister went to live with an aunt in Zembe. She would continue with her schooling at Kamanga.

The first thing I had to do after settling in at Kolomo Camp was to track down my uncle Chimba. He had not replied to any of my letters. Which had disappointed me. But folks who were coming back to Zembe for short periods told us how difficult it was to get to see a government man, let alone talk to him. We were told he was always protected by a number of European secretaries and typists and some severe-looking

African clerks, who were full of airs. All the same I felt offended. He is my asibweni after all.

I tried several times. I got fed up and decided to look for his home address. I would simply go to his house in Kabulonga suburb. That is how I was brought up, damn it! But I made one last desperate effort to go to the government offices — in Transport House. This time I simply punched through the corridors and offices and made direct for his office. To hear things rattle and papers rustle and white women and African clerks with glasses hiss and shout in whispers behind me, you would have thought a small whirlwind had thrown up their skirts and left sand in their mouths and eyes. I managed to reach the real secretary's office. I rattled off a number of things that had been burning inside me. Once a friend had said to me back home: if you want to irritate a European who does not want to give you the attention you want, begin with something like 'You see Madam (or Sir), it's like this — once I was on a mountain and I heard a cry . . .' Just go on, as if you had all the time in the world, before you tell her what you really want. She is bound to do something worthwhile just to be rid of you. The trick worked.

Asibweni proceeded to tell me how I should *not* expect offices to work — I must forget that I have a relative in government. 'I need a job, asibweni.' He was so full of office power as he sat there behind a huge desk with a glass top. He looked at me through the dark pools which lay beneath his forehead. Like a baboon keeping watch from the top of a rock. Full of power, a man with a heavy shadow. There was a large poster on the wall advertising the game park: pictures of giraffe and kudu and so on. On the desk was a large colour photo of a woman. It was not a picture of mai wamung'ono Tirenje. I almost asked if that was a relative of his, but something told me not to. I did not know whether I was meant to make myself at home or not. At the same time I felt proud to have an uncle who was actually a government man.

That is how I came to work for the Loco in Chimba Chirundu's Ministry — Transport and Public Works. In quicker time than I had reckoned, I obtained a driver's licence and became a government driver.

Asibweni asked me to take him to Ambuye Mutiso. They had not met since my mother's funeral. It had begun to rain when we arrived in Kolomo.

'You young men have great work to do,' Ambuye said, holding on to Chimba's hand, so that my uncle had to squat. 'Keep on the right way, you have taken the veil from off our eyes, but you must teach our young ones like Moyo here how to see things. When they say *kwacha!*

they must mean what the word says — it is time to wake up because it is a bright new day. May the ancestors guide you my son.'

'I consider words from your mouth Ambuye as a blessing themselves,' asibweni said gravely, his face seeming to catch a flicker of Ambuye's age in the candlelight. Outside it was raining hard.

I went to the Chirundu house in Kabulonga soon after noon — knocking-off time on Saturdays. I knocked at the door until my knuckles hurt. At last I bunched up a fist and hammered the door. A woman's face peered through a hole in the door. She opened. 'Don't you know how to ring a bell?' she asked in Chinyanja. I looked up and round and could not see a bell. I just barely managed to check my urge to laugh. Why should any one want to hang a bell on the veranda or in the yard, as if he were running a school or church!

'Here-here-here!' the woman said testily. I shrugged my shoulders.

'Yes who do you want?'

'Mr Chimba Chirundu.'

'The Minister of Transport?'

'Yes — Mr Chirundu.'

'Is he expecting you? Why don't you see him at his office?'

These city people — what manners! I thought. *Badly brought up! Hei, I've seen that face before.*

'He is my asibweni.'

'Oh — you must be er — er Moyo?'

'Inde.'

'Come in. Hei, my dear! Here is your nephew! Er — sit down anywhere, I'll go call him.'

Of course, the photo on his desk!

She was tall and slender — too much so for my taste. She had thickly painted black eyebrows. She was dressed casually, for the house, in one of those short above-the-knees dresses. *Her knees will need a wheel-alignment job. Where's Tirenje? Where's mai wamung'ono? What is taking place here?*

'Greetings mupwa!' he said, coming down the stairs.

'Greetings asibweni!' *He's not happy to see me — that's plain on his face.*

'Er — Monde — this is Moyo, my nephew who works for me now. Moyo, this is Miss Lundia.'

'Can I give you a beer?' she asked in a lazy voice, smiling, like a giver of good things. I wondered what I had said to raise a smile, but I didn't try to think much on it.

'It's like this,' asibweni said, frowning slightly as he swallowed a mouthful, 'as I told you the other day — my father had two wives — my grandfather whom I never knew, had had four. Moyo's mother was the child of the first wife, and my own mother was the second wife. Two of my six brothers are still alive, the others died. Moyo's mother was the only child of her mother. She died.'

Your father — my grandfather who did not want my father to marry his daughter. You do not despise Tumbuka like your father, asibweni — you married Nyanja — did you despise my father because he was Tumbuka? Do you despise me because I have Tumbuka blood? Where is Tirenje where is mai wamung'ono where is she?

Miss Lundia continued to nod and smile, like a giver of good things. 'Miss Lundia here has been to England,' asibweni was saying, 'she studied to be a secretary there.' *He does not mention Tirenje at all... where is mai wamung'ono?*

'Would you like a beef sandwich?' Miss Lundia asked, 'we do not cook lunch on Saturdays because the cook is off, I'm sorry.'

'Er-er-yes, no.'

'Sure?'

'Yes thank you.' *These city people — can't they give you food without asking you first if you want it? Sandwich for lunch — ha! A big eater like me . . .*

She continued to smile, like a giver of good things.

When I told Ambuye about my visit he nodded, moved his jaws and said, 'That is the way of the world child of my son. I am too old to be surprised. I remember his father as a very hard man. He did not want your mother to be married to someone outside the Bemba or Lunda people. They have always thought low of us Tumbuka and spat when they spoke of us as cowards. You make slaves out of people because you think low of them, but you really begin to hate them because you have enslaved them — you know they are like scorpions — your mother did not ever want to see her father again — I do not even know why he troubled himself to come to her burial — you know I could not remember whàt this Chimba was like until he came to see me the other day — if he has taken after his father may the gods help him.'

'Can he have left Tirenje? He was very uneasy this afternoon.'

Ambuyę did not seem to hear my question at all. He just mumbled something like '*Sato* is running amok — a god has been smoked out of his den — now he is abroad bringing people's houses down in broad daylight — in the fullness of a bright day — I am too old to understand —

when *sato* drags his weight among people then you know there's something the ancestors want to tell us — something has gone wrong.'

'And I am too young to go into the affairs of the Chirundu house. Something smells bad in that house I cannot know what it is where it lies.'

I had to write a letter to my sister and also to the Elephant on behalf of Ambuye before going to bed.

'I've joined the College of Adult Education,' I told asibweni.

'That's very good mupwa, very good. Finishing your high school?'

'At twenty-two? Oh no. I must learn things that will improve my position where I am.'

'You still need a full high school certificate.'

'No — I'm interested in trade unions — that's what I must spend my evenings reading and studying.'

'Trade unions — what!' I might have told him a donkey had given birth to a pig, the way he jumped. He looked at me as if he didn't trust his hearing.

'That's politics. What do you want to mess with politics for at your age — instead of preparing your mind for bigger things while your brain can still take in and keep the things you learn?'

'You are in politics yourself asibweni — I do not understand. Besides if politics is mixed up with the trade union movement then I must simply accept the fact. I'm not intending to become a Cabinet Minister or Permanent Secretary.'

'Stupid, stupid — you don't even know what city life is like! Take an uncle's advice — stay out of the thing! I think you're being plain stupid!'

I could not understand the reason for Chimba's strong language, his fury. He simply seemed to lose his head. He touched a paper and a pen and dropped them and stood up and stomped up and down behind his desk. I just could not read him.

'If you want to talk anymore about the subject I don't want to hear!' He took his seat again like a man who had been pulled down with a violent jerk when he had stood up to speak at a meeting.

I had made up my mind. The school fees were low, and there was a whole course being offered on the labour movement. When I thought about it, I felt this was one of the ways in which I could keep pace with the demands of city life. Later, after the time of fire and blood that was to follow, something told me that I must have been driven by the same urge that makes a seed push and strain and burst into the world of sun and air and still push and strain in an upward thrust to gain more height.

This was how I came to meet Dr Letanka and grow to love him so much. He taught the course. I plunged headlong into the thing. Once in it I knew it was the direction my life would have to take. It could not be otherwise. Dr Letanka was a South African who was teaching in a project begun and supported by an international organization for economic growth in Africa. I found out from him, as we became friends, that he had left South Africa so that he could teach what he liked and as he felt it should be done, not as it was ordered by the white government of that country.

'In fact,' Dr Letanka told me, 'I was trained in mathematics and my doctorate was in that area. I hunted for a job for months in British universities, but no dice. All the English ever want a black man to teach at university is anthropology or an African language. So I took a part-time job in a small technical high school in Manchester. Meantime I decided to study privately for the M.A. in history, specializing in what I am teaching now. But it was mostly because I had come to love history.'

'That fellow was a wizard in mathematics,' Pitso told me during one of my visits in jail. 'Hoo, a wizard, man. No one could touch him. But he had no place in those white universities, no place that he deserved in the black college full of Boers. And he had had the whole damn fraud up to here. Believe me, I went to the same black college — same class with his younger brother. Hell man, a wizard, wooo!'

I believed Pitso. The doctor was not any less brilliant in history.

'I asked him if he had a family,' I said to Pitso, 'and he brushed the question aside.'

'Well, he has a wife and three children in England. Now don't go blabbing about it to anyone — hear?'

'Trust me.'

'He loves this place although it gives him much pain too, like it does us. Hardly misses a dance or cocktail or a late night party. Sometimes I'm afraid for him. I mean even from what he tells me and Chieza about his party-going. You see it in his face — something — something — how shall I say? You know — like he wants to eat up life in big juicy chunks and leave nothing behind — chew bones offal and all.'

'What makes you fear for him?'

'Don't know, man — just seems like — like he's tearing downhill all the time and you could break your neck goin' at that speed — and after all, you can eat as much time as you want — it'll still go on after you're six feet down.'

I shrugged my shoulders. I admired 'Studs', as everybody who knew him called him — admired him too much to want to worry about him. Who was I to judge if a man's love for a good time was dangerous or not? But little did I guess that the meaning of Pitso's words would come home with the rude jolt it did. It was to leave us all stunned and numb.

'He was not nicknamed Studs for nothing back home,' Pitso said. 'He loved good expensive studs and cuff links, almost the way a man loves a woman or alcohol. Of course there was a whole bunch of African snobs on the faculty, especially before the Boers began to run it. Ask him about it — he'll tell it you willingly.'

A slender man with an eager-looking face, bulging eyes, slight balding on the head, an explosive raucous laugh that came from deep down in the bowels. Such a man was Studs. His frank face put you at ease with him. You could not ever imagine that he could chew your buttocks off when you were not looking. When he said, 'I despise schemers and rumour-mongers,' you could not but believe him.

This was the man Chimba accused of plotting or setting our workers against the government — no, against the Minister of Transport himself — of helping us revive a labour union for government drivers and mechanics. Letanka's life was too busy and full for him to find time to mess with local politics. His employers would fire him for such conduct anyhow. He was too intelligent and sensitive to destroy his own base.

It was he who introduced me to the prisoners Pitso and Chieza. We often took turns to visit them, to take them newspapers and other reading materials. I felt my life broaden, my feelings deepen, in their company. It was Letanka's teaching that fired me and my co-worker Sikota to begin shaking up the Government Transport Workers Union, in order to bring it back to life. It had been a mere paper organization, with nothing it could call funds or officials. The workers were ripe for it. They elected me secretary, being one of about three men with three years of high school. Without personally attending any meetings at all Studs gave us a number of ideas to work on. But he did not use the class time to do this. We had reason to be proud of what we were making: the workers were so keen, so alert. We realized that one of the first things we would have to attack fiercely was suspicion and distrust between Bemba, Lozi, Tumbuka, Tonga, Nyanja and so on.

Nights when I lay in bed, with Ambuye a few feet away from me breathing hard, I thought about all the things that had happened to me,

that had come into me, that opened up my mind — my whole being —
so that my heart ached to know more, to stretch out, to conquer I
knew not what. I toyed with the idea that Ambuye must be listening to
my thoughts and longings when he turned over on his mat . . .

'A trade union must not be content simply to press the employers to
pay better wages, to produce better working conditions,' Dr Letanka
would say in class. 'These are very important, yes. But it must also interest itself in the schooling, medical care, general social welfare of the
workers — several other things that are related to the quality and size of
what the worker produces . . .'

He invited me and Sikota for a drive around the townships of the
capital. 'I want to show you something,' Studs said. 'We are leaving the
centre of the city now — we're moving into the suburbs where only
whites used to live in colonial days — civil servants, merchants, messeng-
ers of overseas commercial houses — the lot . . . See the good houses,
big yards because they had servants galore they could keep for very
little money — there are three of these suburbs — see the streets are
clean, see the avenues of trees, the parks . . . there's the Bristol Club —
wherever the English go they must have a club — if they were on safari
across the desert the first tent they pitched would be a club . . . used to
keep out Africans, the Bristol, now they let them in at a high membership fee only civil servants and company gentlemen can afford . . .
there's the International School — for foreign children . . . the Cabinet
Ministers' children go there today, so high the fees are . . . supposed to
give a first-class education — all in English of course . . . You say why
don't foreign children go to public schools and the big nobs say the
teaching there is poor, the classes crowded . . . man — man — by God! . . .
They also tell you the country would lose foreign services . . . You say
look man, these people live in clover here they've run away from over-
crowded houses and high taxes and cut-throat competition — it's no
sacrifice for them here — why create a school that sets children of rich
folks apart from the rest? . . . Now we go to the poor housing . . . This
is where the Africans were tucked away — in City Council houses —
two-roomed boxes as you see — the city fathers are adding more to
them, more and still more and quite apart from those suburbs where
the new middle class has taken over . . . The teacher, labourer, church
minister, burglar, driver — they live here . . . yes if you must have servants, those are the people who must open for the burglars, even help
take the loot themselves . . . Now where you are Moyo, there you have
nests of burglars, but they only use Kolomo, Kalingalinga, Chelston —

all those pockets of poverty — as a base — they sell to those who live here, like in your township, Sikota . . . You should know.'

'That is where I plan to move to,' I said, 'where Sikota lives. It's a better place, I may even get to buy one of your chairs or shirts or blankets, Dr Letanka.'

'Be my guest — but be warned. I'll still go to the police and they may trace them to you.'

'And if you don't speak their tongue,' Sikota remarked, 'they'll do nothing.'

'If you think we must have burglars, how'd you feel about them if they broke into your house?' I asked Dr Letanka.

'Same as everybody else. To say we'll always have burglars because there are other people who have a lot to be stolen doesn't mean I'm prepared to give a thief a medal. But that's not my point in taking you places just now. After all Sikota knows this city better than I do — it's your country. What I'd ask you both to be thinking about are those conditions a trade union will have to concern itself with once the organization has been operating. Schools, clinics, hospitals, houses, parks, community halls, markets, class divisions — see, it's a big thing you've started.'

He paused for a spell. We sat there in his car, all three of us dead quiet, as if we were waiting for one of us to speak — or anything. He cleared his throat and said, 'Now then, I've left Kabwata township last because something is happening there I was invited to — I don't know if I should go — the thing has been tossing about in my mind — I was trying to buy time — I hoped by now I'd have made up my mind one way or the other.' He paused again, then suddenly, 'Damn it — it's a few houses down the street — if you decide to come in with me fine, if not, I'll take you home first.'

Sikota and I looked at each other. What was he talking about I wondered? Before I could ask we were in front of the house. The sound of a church hymn filtered into the still night. A man came up to us from the direction the car was facing. As he passed under a light on the pavement it was quite clear that he had had plenty to drink. He shaded his eyes with his hand, bent over to the driver's side. 'Heit, Bra Studs!' the man said, clearly happy he had recognized Dr Letanka.

'Heit O-Duke!'

'Woozet, Bra Studs?'

'Straight, man, and you?'

'So-so. Hei, Bra Studs, how about a kwacha dere — hic — just one —

I want to collect — hic — at our brother's wake — hic — in dere — you know — Bra Mojo has got a wake for his late mother — hic — all the folks is in dere — please Bra Studs.'

'Now look, O-Duke,' Dr Letanka said, hissing like some dangerous creature, which gave me a start, 'I have a kwacha — if you wanted to buy food or even a drink I'd give it to you — really I would but not for this kind of game — sorry mate!' Dr Letanka started the car and shot forward, throwing us a good few inches back as we had moved to the edge of the seats.

'Sorry — sorry, boys,' he said, panting with anger. 'That chap back there got stuck in my gullet but made the decision for me.'

'What is all that singing about?' Sikota asked.

'This fellow, Mojo, is an exile from Johannesburg and lives in England. Gets a grant from an American Foundation — so we're told — who knows for sure? — he gets a grant to come and do research into religious sects for a book. Well, he throws parties and he's seen in just too many gay places for a man in his job. He gets news from Jo'burg his mother has died. What does he do? — invites the refugees here to a wake in a friend's house —'

'So he can collect money?' I put in.

'Well, you heard Duke with your own ears.'

'Do you think he won't send the money home?'

'He has no people left in the family — but on the other hand he may send it to those relatives who buried his mother — but maybe that's not what really bothers me — no, it does — what's kicking around inside me with a louder noise is that we're tired of being asked to funerals without corpses — *I* am anyhow.'

Funerals without corpses, funerals without corpses . . . The words turned over and over in my mind . . .

'I'll take you home now, friends. We three come from a long history — lots and lots of it still waiting to be written — empires wars slavery Europeans tradition custom — heroes we must have — we must remember — we must know where we came from to understand where we are where we're going — we must remember — that's a tremendous gift — memory — you know what I mean? Not to forget. But we cannot now hold ceremonies over the millions dead and gone during the long journey in slavery — the journey across the seas. Memory should strengthen us, it should not detain us in the funeral parlour or at the graveside — it gets tiresome to have to keep going to funerals without corpses — *I am tired,* God! It's what Mojo's doing gets me off on my pet subject.'

After classes my head swam and what Dr Letanka said to us became enlarged in my mind to a size that frightened me, made me wonder if a little voice in me had not misled me. Was I fit to take on such a task — I mean to join in it? The little voice said to me 'Hold on, Moyo, stay on the job . . .' It seemed the gates behind me had been closed and there was no going back . . .

Studs also took me to parties. 'You've got to see and know what makes life in this city,' he said. 'By the time I'm through with you you'll be so mixed up you won't know whether you're seeing stars through the arse of a hippo, eh?'

The moment we entered a house Studs would quickly mix with the guests as if he knew every one of them. Of course he must have. 'This is not a big town,' he would reply to my question, 'and the same people get to meet at most parties. But the VIP parties -- huh — that's another story altogether. You won't know whom you've met before — all diplomats are alike. There I can't take you I'm sorry to say — you've got to have a card damn it. But I'll sneak you in one of these days. Just pretend you're as stuck up as those undertakers are and you'll pass — it's time you knew important people in and out of their offices with and without wives and concubines — see what I mean?'

'Yes professor.'

'By God!' Studs would continually exclaim. Then you knew he was just where he loved to be — dancing or telling a story or listening to one or tasting a drink or swallowing it. He drank heavily, but always turned up to his evening classes as if nothing had happened the night before.

He took me to parties made by American Embassy people. I found out that there were two kinds of American parties: one which would be attended by the ambassador etcetera, which important leaders of freedom movements in exile would attend in addition to the diplomatic nobs; then there was another kind made by a junior officer in the embassy -- cultural attaché or someone dealing with passports and visas. Here would be found the rank and file of the refugee type as well as other unpretentious folk. One such embassy officer was a timid little man who did nothing but smoke his pipe at a party, drinking himself silly. He had a wife who was full of bosom and bounce who twisted shamelessly in the middle of the floor, out of beat, like the tail of a lizard that has been cut off from the body. She had a passion for African males, so rumour had it. 'My kingdom for a pink mare!' Studs would say when she did her motions on the dance floor — 'God!'

Once we left unusually early. Studs invited me to his apartment. 'Let's go and drink in some peace and quiet for a change. I need company.' When we arrived he said, 'This is my hole, Moyo — this is my hole.' He threw himself on the sofa. Then he put beer and scotch and glasses on the small table. His eyes looked very sad. I could not remember when last I had seen such sad eyes.

'Had a letter today from my wife in England,' he said.

'I hope she's well — and the children?'

'Oh there'll never be anything the matter with them. Whew, it's an angry letter — man, has that woman got a helluva sting to her pen! Cheers to our friendship!'

'Cheers!'

'You are the first person I tell this. I wouldn't trust any of my countrymen — the colony of refugees we've got here — they are all frustrated men. Thought they would march back home in quick time and it's eight years already since some of them were out — they start scratching themselves and backbiting each other and fighting in taverns because they're afraid to answer back when your people insult them — turning around in circles or deserting · you see how they hate themselves and become mean — how could I confide in any one all these five years I've been here? God, have they got troubles!'

'Don't be uneasy — I know you're thinking I am about double your age and you're still too tender to carry grave matters like these. But damn it you're a man and you're already taking on big things — you're going to learn age counts for mosquito shit — nothing — in politics.'

Indeed I felt awkward, but in his presence this did not last. I had a number of questions to ask, but I let him talk. He spoke slower than was his usual way. Except when words would come out in torrents, as if falling over each other . . .

'I graduated in mathematics at Fort Hare College in my country — you've heard of it? —'I'm sure. A good few of your Cabinet Ministers got their B.A.s there. I had a talent for mathematics -- it often terrified me because the other students treated me as if I were a genius dropped from heaven — they were not at ease in my company. Anyhow, when we were still allowed to enter English-medium universities I went to the one in Johannesburg to do the doctorate. I went back to teach at Fort Hare where I had left my wife and two children. A beautiful woman — those days -- met when we were both students — daughter of a court interpreter — a big name in that area. If ever you get to read Booker T. Washington — you know the American negro who wrote *Up from Slav-*

ery? — sure, you must have heard about it at least — I've seen a copy in the United States Information reading room in town — about the only kind of thing they keep by American blacks — Oh, I'm going off the subject — but what did I begin to say? — Yes, also *Ebony* magazine — anything that talks about American blacks who've achieved a social status above the manual labourer or the messenger — that Fort Hare community was like that. Mark you, with more English teachers than Africans, some of us sincerely felt they had arrived — their wives fussed about the kind of furniture and crockery they should have — whispered and laughed among themselves about those other women who had no desire to compete — loved to be invited by European women for afternoon tea — all that stupid stuff. They were also teaching their children to speak English at home and pushing their daughters into ballet classes — my God! A rising elite with no money, no land. I must admit I myself began to feel I had arrived. At the end of the forties when young nationalists — many of them are the ones on Robben Island or living in exile — when enlightened nationalism exploded, those who spoke the Mister-and-Missus-request-the-pleasure-of etcetera kind of language got a rude shock. I was still too busy with my doctorate then — no, that's a flat excuse — I'm not the political type — when I joined the staff they'd settled back to their empty little parish amusements. My wife was in the thick of it — all those families who had become a kind of upper class without political or real economic power — a long tradition of education was all they could brag about — and of course white liberal aid — without some white missionary signing their testimonials they'd have had to claw their own way up the ladder — you see, I was from the slum ghettoes of the gold mining areas up country — my time of studying in Johannesburg was a kind of refresher course in slum living — when I returned to Fort Hare I couldn't stomach it — couldn't take all that piano-decorated, suit-and-tie culture — all that made me feel actually sick in body. My wife wouldn't leave because she was so locked up in her fat family name, so attached to her mother. She was ruthless with faculty wives she despised. Something inside told me to be reckless. I fell in love with a teacher in a local primary school — a lovely girl of ordinary peasant upbringing — made her pregnant — so the missionary board of the college simply had to expel me — the only way I could have uprooted my family from that life. Could have gone back to any of the new colleges but they're run by — ahem-you-know-what — fellows who have replaced the missionaries and have their own idea of what kind of education my people must have, and I'd have to be screened. They're allergic to efficiency and scholastic merit, if you see what I mean. First stop was England and jobs for blacks are not easy to come by in those universities — the only blacks limeys can stand in their institutions are those who can teach ethnology or anthropology or some African language. I had hoped I could apply for a job in an African university through the London recruiting officer — I just couldn't understand it, never could get through. I was trapped. Anyway, in those cold years in that cold society I realized my wife and I had drifted a long distance apart. We had a third child now and they were all in high school. I found a teaching job in mathematics in some small technical college in Yorkshire — kept me alive, that's all it did. She never forgave me for pulling her out of that precious set at home — wouldn't open the door some nights — because the way you drink disgusts me, she said . . . what would your friends at Fort Hare think to see you like this? — she would say. Of course I did drink more than I'd ever done before. Gave her a nasty beating once, which I've ever regretted since. But I never drank so much I couldn't function. What friends? My God! — those were not friends — those sausages from the mission-school machine could never be my friends. I reminded her — I had a friend from up country whose wife you couldn't stand because you said she was ordinary — soon my friend joined the pack too and his wife died a very lonely woman. You know what she says to me? She says if it weren't for me you'd have gone back to those slums you came from — by God! — that woman, *that woman!* A semi-rural girl like her who just happened to be the daughter of a court interpreter who had powerful connections with the board controlling Fort Hare. Made me sweat in my arse when she said that. After seven years of that frozen life in England I decided I had had it. I should have known it long before — but you know, Moyo, there's a way Christian teaching sinks into your bones when you let it because you need good testimonials from the white missionary to get ahead in employment, because we are a whole fuckin' nation of teachers nurses and church ministers, we blacks in South Africa — if you're not a manual labourer or messenger-filing-clerk — and so you need that testimonial so bad and at the end of the passage the white man you're asking to hire you goes by the word of his white brother-in-Christ and there you are smack between two fellows who have planned to keep you running. Painful thing is you know it but there's fuckall you can do about it — you've got to survive — you know, when those Boers took over that College and set up their tribal kindergarten colleges they talked like they really believed the missionaries — all those desperate spin-

sters and bachelors and grey-heads — were teaching us revolution. No —
what scared them is that the missionaries simply let us learn — thought
if they set their minds on making Christians out of us we'd never turn
violent, we'd always obey the law. But the Boers wanted to use chains
and two-legged bloodhounds to control our minds — castrate us — a
method that would positively stop rebellion — you can say at least the
missionary stuff left us open to other influences. But I'm rambling —
the scotch is playing around inside of me — but I was going to say the
Church bores into you with that sense of guilt — I should have divorced
her but kept thinking it would be a sin, I'd be damned — you see I was
raised Anglican. So I felt if I was going to hell at all it should be for a
very good reason — because I had dared to enjoy life. I longed to be
back in the slums where my people are — connect again — wipe off all
that cream-of-society bunk — be myself again. So here I am, there you
are.'

'What about the children?' I interrupted for the first time.

He shook his head slowly. 'Those! Their mother has taught them
English habits — my daughter once pulled me up for laughing aloud in
the street — in Liverpool. No, they have grown to despise me. I've a lot
to blame myself for — where I should have been tough and firm I didn't
take control of things in the family. In this she is stronger than me — oh
that woman is strong — I envy her for that. You have one person — her
— who is strong and obstinate even when she's wrong, and another person — me — who loves his freedom and leaves himself open for change
and so relaxes his grip — because — because — how shall I put it? — my
head was buried so long in mathematics, I was terrified by my own ability to work with figures, equations, problems and swore to myself never
to deal with human beings like that — no, I'm not saying a tenth of
what I really feel. But here I am, there you are. Zora as you know is an
office typist from Zimbabwe who loves life herself — lives in an ordinary Council house — a real woman, not a paper woman — hei, I must
ask her to introduce you to her friend — a beauty — decent girl too —
you can't be muckin' around alone without a good woman. Her name is
Nachele.'

'I'll try it.'

Yes, Studs was running away from something, looking for something
better, I was doing just that myself. So was Chimba; so was Pitso too,
who wanted to return to the south; a man whose nerves had given in,
who had grown bulky, had a bad ulcer, was known for his long deep si-

lences — here he was, bent on returning to the torture cells out of which he had escaped. So was Chieza, who was bent on waiting behind prison bars. Studs kept up a breathlessly busy life, always hungry, it seemed to me, for more and more . . . I could not even feel sorry for him: he did not seem to need it, he seemed so free, so full of vitality. And yet again it was quite clear he was looking for something that could tie him to the earth and all that goes with it — the clay, the dust, the manure, the dead leaves, the bugs, the worms, the rocks, the water . . . I asked him what his wife said in this last letter. He dismissed the question with a wave of the hand. A letter from her was a very rare thing, he explained. He sent her money for their living every month. I tried hard to picture in my mind the kind of woman she might be — beyond what he told me: what kind of heart she might have. I gave up. Whoever knows what really goes on in married people's hearts that makes them turn against each other, I thought to myself — or makes one of them run and run and run and clear so many miles?

A letter from my sister arrived. She was doing well at school. She wanted to come to the capital to study nursing. I encouraged her.

I met Nachele through Zora. Not anything like Zora. She was more steady and quieter. Her very bright eyes made my voice tremble a bit. when I first spoke to her. She did not make it easy for me to talk to her. You like it in this city? Yes, she answered. And your typing job? Yes. You travel by bus? Yes. Do you like to go to the stadium to watch football? No. What do you like to do in your free time? Visit with people. And so on it would go. I can't make people laugh, she couldn't say anything to make me laugh. When Zora was present, talk became freer, more lively.

We became closer as time went on. 'So many things make you laugh,' she would say. And yet I realized there were fewer things to make me laugh. 'You should have known me back home in Zembe,' I would say. Yes, something was happening to me . . .

Only Ambuye Mutiso was not looking for anything any longer. He was always arguing with Old Wina who lived three houses up the alley. They kept each other company during the day. I was glad this could happen. Old Wina would keep repeating, 'I told them,' meaning his son and daughter-in-law with whom he lived, 'I told them they must take my lifeless body home to bury it — I do not want to be buried in this heap of rubbish — I want to be with my Lozi ancestors, you hear me Mutiso?'

'Your ancestors are everywhere in this land, son of Wina, ask *me* — I am Tumbuka and I have wandered many years — are you saying I should be carried all the way to Malawi? You must have lost your head.'

'You have lost your head yourself if you — if you —' And Old Wina would splutter and take his snuff and not finish what he was saying.

They argued about chiefs, how the young men in government were counting them out of the nation's affairs except as puppets. Ambuye would tease his friend, as if he disagreed, but they would end the discussion in complete accord.

Ambuye took ill. In three-four days he was gone. Old Wina wept openly.

Back home the old men and women would have come to wash the corpse and prepare it for burial. Wina's son told me how things were done in the city. A local carpenter made a coffin and we took it to the hospital. We sat on the coffin in the black van. The doctors gave us a death certificate and the body waited in the mortuary. The body was carried in a sheet into a small room at the corner of the cemetery grounds and laid on the concrete floor. The sheet was removed. A stench — eleven cubic feet of it — clung to the air in that room. The floor must have been always wet, the way I saw it. A man hosed the body, turning it over with a long stick. I was burning with anger and disgust, so vulgar the whole business looked: that my grandfather should be handled like some animal at a slaughter house. Other corpses that waited in line went through the same treatment. The body was dried, dressed and taken to the grave. The only other people at the graveside were Old Wina's wife, our next-door neighbour, Studs and his woman Zora. Chimba was out of town. Nachele could not leave her job that day.

I turned down an invitation from Studs and Zora to go to their apartment.

I sat in my shack for the rest of the afternoon. Dusk set in, and it took me long to realize that I had not lighted the lamp. I was trying to find out if indeed I wasn't feeling any sense of loss. Or I was trying to feel something. Suddenly after burying him I felt empty inside. No grief, no regret — nothing. I felt ashamed of this. The ancestors would punish me, I thought. How could I just feel nothing about Ambuye, the last man to remind me who I was, where I came from? In the dark the smell of old age came to me. Something I had hardly ever known was there before. Now it seemed to come on heavy, like the very presence of Ambuye. That was when I stood up to light the lamp, my heart beating rather fast. I put out the lamp and walked out towards the bus stop. Just as if it was the most natural thing to do.

I went from one bar to another, wherever the whim took me to alight from a bus: from Lilanda to Matero to Chelston to Mangoni through the bars in the centre of town to Libala. It was malt beer all the way until I took a stiff Scotch in the last two bars. I got off the bus in Kabwata. I stopped on the roadside and looked around, up at the stars, unzipped my fly and let off what felt like a torrent of water, a slight shiver of relief running through me. The lights of what I guessed to be Kabulonga, where the rich ones, the Cabinet Ministers, the company directors etcetera live, fell in my line of vision as my head swung around, as if it wanted to have nothing to do with my body anymore. I remember having shouted something like 'Kabulonga — that's where you are uncle Chimba — asibweni Chimba! I'm not afraid of you — do what you like — I'm going to run my union the way I like — maybe you think because I'm Tumbuka I'm worth little or nothing — I'm coming, you stubborn proud Bemba I'm coming you wait and see! Why did you marry mai wamung'ono Tirenje and then walk over her like that — because she's Nyanja? I've got Ambuye, what have you got? The house of Chirundu is no more, no more — me I've got Ambuye! All you have is that Transport House — you'll eat dust my boy, *sato* will skin you alive — me, I've got Ambuye . . .' A jumble of things of this nature. If I did not say them out loud, they had all the same been crying out for that bold moment when I could say them — and more . . .

I felt sick. I rushed to a storm drain and threw up, there on my knees, shivering from the effort to bring up more, my throat aching. I raised myself and walked through the scantily-lit streets, holding on to an electric pole now and again, looking up through wet eyes at the moths playing stupidly, mindlessly around the bulbs, while I swayed on the pole. I could not remember the next day how I found Nachele's quarters . . .

We must not do anything tonight — you have lost your grandfather we do not do it when there is a death in the family. No, we must not do anything. Nachele's voice had sounded a long long way off, I remembered the next morning. Studs's words came back to me — we're tired of being asked to funerals without corpses — funerals without corpses. We had a funeral for Ambuye so why the phrase? Try as I might to push it off, it would not leave me alone. It irritated me, even frightened me a little, because I felt accused. I remembered also that as I knelt there over the storm drain vomiting, I kept saying *Save me Ambuye save me* — without knowing clearly what it was I wanted to be saved from.

I returned to my shack the next day. I bundled up Ambuye's two blankets, pillow, grass mat and the few items of clothing to send them to the Elephant by country bus. He would know what to do. Had Ambuye died at home, the proper thing to do would have been for one of our relatives to take them after a cleansing, or for them to be buried with him. Move, Moyo, move, I said to myself. Move as soon as you can find a vacant Council house. Go to Libala or Chelston, wherever, but move. My chance came, after two years of waiting. It was to be Kabwata. As the real owner of the shack was not turning up, I left it with a newcomer from Zembe. 'Listen,' I said to him, 'our homeboy comes here only when he wants to hide loot or is in flight. Police are hot here, so he's mostly in the Copperbelt. If he does come, you must be ready to do what you think best.'

I drove Chimba to Shimoni to visit his family. The puzzle grew bigger in my head. But it was not my place to ask questions.

'They have gone to Musoro,' Old Chirundu said.

We headed for Musoro in the east.

Mai wamung'ono was excited to see us. And yet I sensed a deep sadness in her eyes. Almost as if she would cry any moment. Off and on a kind of shadow travelled over her face, as when suddenly a cloud passes under the sun and you can see a shadow moving on the ground, up a slope . . .

She asked for my address, which I gave her.

When she came with the children to the capital to stay, I was all the more mystified. But her presence was some relief to my mind; if only because she did not look rejected and deserted out there in Musoro, away from her husband.

How could I have guessed that Tirenje's coming to the city would begin a train of events that were to break upon us like a tornado? First, I felt like a bumbling idiot after I had agreed to take her to her husband's house — where the other woman reigned. They were like two wild cats determined each to keep the other one out of her territory. Mai wamung'ono went straight to the kitchen, I stood in the hall. Words, bitter ugly words, exploded between them, burning and smoking the air right up to where I was standing. The gardener saved the day, just when they were moving closer for a real fight. It would have been too much for me to try to deal with a quarrel between women their ages.

After this, it did not surprise me that mai wamung'ono should return to Musoro. Asibweni was hardening, growing more and more quick-tempered.

The rains came. When it rains on this plateau, it comes down for four months. Just on and on, letting up only for brief spells. The air is always heavy with water. Even one's spirits, one's mind, seem to soak it up. In the end, after so much rain, one feels humbled, in a strange sort of way. When it rains, Kolomo shanties look sicker than they have ever been before. You think any moment they are going to come down in one heap under the rain. Some do collapse. After the rain people are busy raising poles and knocking on fresh sheets of rusted tin and cardboard and wood and concrete blocks — all on no foundation at all. They have always been told by the City that they are where they are only for the time being . . . Here in Kabwata, one begins to appreciate the misery of Kolomo.

When it rains, my mind travels back to my boyhood in the country. Rope skipping with two boys or girls holding either end and teams jumping all along the ten feet of ground between the 'poles'. Moist earth yielded no dust, the fibre of the rope gathered soil and held it and the added weight made it easier to swing it . . . My mind travels back to the rain mist that hung over a hill or a cliff as if something held it there . . . To the flying ants, to the chorus of insect song . . . To the caked earth by the river that we licked for the sweet salt that had surfaced . . . To many days of plenty and of drought . . . To the life I knew I would never return to. Because deep inside me I had a misty sense that Kolomo was for me a passage to something else, bigger than itself. And when it rains I think of my father and my mother — their courage, their — dare I say defeat? No, I dare not. And yet what was it? Was their failure simply the failure of Kazembe, of this whole land, of history? I cannot be sure.

On a Sunday morning Zora startled me with a visit to my house. 'Studs is in hospital,' she said, breathlessly.

'What's the matter?'

'His car crashed head-on into another.'

'Was he alone?'

'He was with a friend — that one is all right but he cannot remember what happened. They must have been drinking — how many times have I spoken to Studs? — it is too much the way you're drinking, I say to him — drinks never get finished, the man does. All right, I say to him, you go to work and you do all right at school, you're clean, your house is clean, but when you get your hands on drinks it's like you're getting ready to push a building down — oh —'

'Be calm, Zora, be calm — I'm sure he will be all right. What about the other man?'

'Nowhere to be found — just vanished, left his wrecked car. Studs' car is a complete wreck — that's the end of it.'

'That's the end of the case, they'll never go looking for him even when the car licence and everything are there.'

Zora shook her head. She was crying.

'Let us go,' I said.

Studs' spleen had ruptured, so it had to be removed. He had no wounds that one could see, except a fractured leg. After two weeks he seemed to be coming round. He could sit up. His wife came from England. She looked thin and wasted. She did not say much. Just cried softly. Almost all the time, it seemed. And she spent whole days at his bedside — right into the late hours of the night.

When he was sitting up like that, and we were able to talk to him, Studs tried to be jovial. But it was clear that something inside was in the way. I looked at his eyes, and I saw the same deep, terrifying sadness that had struck me the night he told me the events of his life. My mood sank. He seemed to be moving away and away even from his wife — if she had ever reached him since she arrived. He would pause in the middle of a sentence, as if listening to a fault in the engine deep down inside.

The doctors said pus was dripping from some organ or other, they were trying to check it. His liver was not healthy. Jaundice set in. In the fourth week Studs died. His widow cried aloud and on and on, and her frail-looking body looked as if it would crumble any moment, just dissolve. She took the corpse back to England. I could not find the connection between what Studs had told me and the manner his death hit her. I couldn't. I fell back on the thought that we would never really know how it had all begun, what precisely went wrong. What he had told me could not explain it all. I felt his death deep down in my being — but words are a waste of death . . .

'We cannot allow this in a free country like ours. Two Portuguese spies enter our country after their masters in Portugal have ordered the bombing of our villages. We are told there has been a mistrial, they have to be tried again. These judges are doing the same thing they used to do when we were a colony. Let them resign! I call upon the Youth Brigade to march to the courts and demonstrate!'

The President of the country had spoken.

The Youth Brigade got ready to march.

Our strike had begun. Our men and women were picketing the Government Buildings and Parliament House and the Loco yards.

The Youth Brigade, headed by the crazy Minister, trooped up Mulungushi Drive towards the Court Building.

They crashed in and turned tables and benches and filing cabinets upside-down. They busted the cabinets and removed court records and burned them in a heap on the front steps.

The President said on the radio that he was shocked by this behaviour. This was not what he had told the Brigade to do.

The crazy Minister made himself heard: 'Burn down all neo-colonial institutions and we'll build new ones!'

The judge and the Chief Justice ran into a nearby church until it was dark enough for them to sneak out.

The Youth Brigade marched to the university. They convinced the greater part of the student body that they ought to join in with them. The Portuguese had to be lynched, they shouted.

On their way to the prison they took our strikers with them. We had warned our strikers against violence. They had to show that our cause was serious, violence would reduce it to a game.

It seemed they could not resist the mighty push of such a large body of brigaders and students.

Police cordoned off the prison.

Meantime my executive was trying to get the message across to the Permanent Secretary of Transport and Public Works, Secretary to the Cabinet and the Minister of Justice that our strikers were forced to join the mob. Chimba, of course, was in jail.

Night was upon the city. The moon was bright enough for one to see a louse, as we say.

Having failed to enter the prison, and after a few skulls had been broken, three or four bodies felled by gunshots, two or three necks broken by water from a giant hose, the crowd turned toward State House, the President's residence.

A wagon full of buckets of human manure was towed by tractor right through the fence enclosing the State House grounds. Men tipped over the contents of the wagon on the lawn, as near the back entrance of the building as they could get. Wagon, tractor and buckets were abandoned on the spot.

We could smell the manure from our office in town. And the moon was bright.

Transport House was on fire.

Damn them, damn these crude no-count brigaders! we cursed. Of all the things to do! Why can't that crazy Minister control the monsters? we kept asking.

Slum rats! The records of all the affairs of the Ministry of Transport and Public Works — imagine! And with the kind of fire station we have!

Damn the slum rats!

The strike must go on! Kwacha!

Yes! Kwacha!

We're claiming our rights! Kwacha!

Yes! Kwacha!

Let's keep cool heads — those brigaders and students must not break the strike!

No! Kwacha!

Tomorrow they'll be going back to university, on comfortable government scholarships — money from our taxes . . .

Yes they will have forgotten us the labourers!

They're on the way to middle class!

Yes — they're comfortable — all they're having is fun . . .

You're right — else why did they wait for the Youth Brigade to tell them what to do? Why did they not join our strike in the first place?

They keep complaining about food and dormitories and all that heap of dung instead of working hard and finishing studies so they could come out and help us . . .

A man came into the union office, out of breath, and drew me aside. It was Chimba's gardener. He lived in an outhouse for servants on Chimba's property. His wild eyes told me —

'My son, your uncle's house is on fire — the new house!'

'What!'

'True as my father lies in his grave — your asibweni's wife — the new one — left the house and sent the cook and the cleaner away — she said her life was not safe alone while the strike was on — I said I will stay — what can they do to an old man like me? — now I took a short nap in my room — I was going to lock the house later — I was woken up by sounds of crackling — I jumped up and this knee slowed me down and I saw smoke and flames shoot out of the windows — outside under the light in the yard towards the gate — in the moonlight — I saw her standing there like a stone — these two eyes are old but her face was clear — it was your mai wamung'ono — your uncle's real wife — she did not move — she just stood there and when I went close she said it is finished — then she left.

I reasoned in my mind that all the police must have rushed to the main event of the day, so the house must have been gutted.

'I do not want to get mixed up with this and have to stand in court and be scolded by those youngsters who tie ropes round you with the white man's language pointing a finger at me — nobody — I saw nobody there you hear me son? — I saw no one there I just saw fire — if you tell anyone I told you all this I will say you are lying you hear me well son?'

'I hear old man, I hear.'

I knew there was nothing to be gained by running around asking for a lift to the house.

'Where will you sleep, old father?'

'I have a relative in Matero.'

'Here, take this for your bus fare.'

Indeed the morning paper reported, among other things, that Chimba's new house had been razed to the ground. The police were going to question Monde whenever they could locate her. It was assumed that the rioters had set it on fire . . .

Later in the morning the President escorted the Chief Justice and the judge who killed the sentence on the Portuguese to the airport.

Questions were asked about this kind of courtesy. No one gave answers — no one who mattered.

When I went to collect Tirenje and her cousin to help them with their loads for the bus, mai wamung'ono said to me, 'Mupwa, it is still early, let us sit down a little. You have many big things to do and the ancestors of Mutiso's house will give you strength. I am sure the next time we meet you will be married, perhaps you will even be the father of a daughter or a son, eh? Me, I am going to begin again, I will build another house. Hear me mupwa, I am not afraid anymore. Once I was struck dumb with terror looking at a python kill a goat. The next time I saw *nsato* I was a woman — just before I lost a little thing I was carrying — this time I was not afraid. *Nsato* could not hurt anyone. But when *nsato* leaves his lair to molest and murder human beings the world is upside down, it is a wicked thing it must be destroyed — it must be put in a cage and its den burned down. You are a man now you know what I mean — if your heart tells you to report this about the house to your uncle, do so — if it tells you to hold your tongue, let it be so. The old gardener saw me — he can also tell his master if he is so moved.'

'He came to tell me, mai wamung'ono, he will not tell. Me, I could not even if I wanted to — something tells me I cannot, I do not know what it is.'

'Do not promise, mupwa, only listen to your heart, you hear me? Yes.'

'Go in peace, mai wamung'ono. You know where I live. We should be leaving now.'

The President ordered that no charges should be brought against anybody. Indeed I do not know how the police could nail down anybody at all out of all that mighty crowd, in all that confusion.

'I must warn anybody who takes the law in their own hands next time they behave that way my government will deal with them in the sternest way possible. It has never happened in the history of any African country I know of that the President's office was so disgraced by filthy-minded ruffians capable of pouring human manure on State property. That is *your* property, not mine. I am President but if you don't want to show *me* respect, retain your sense of decency towards the *office* that your Constitution has created and to which you elected me. As for the strike, I have ordered another round of negotiations, but I am hereby, as your President, ordering you back to work. Those who do not comply with this order by tomorrow noon, twenty-four hours from now, must consider themselves fired. I commend the strike leaders for their publicized efforts to suppress violence and vandalism among their followers. As for the students, I have ordered the university to close down forthwith. Everyone who wants to return must re-apply and sign a pledge not to repeat the disgraceful conduct we have just witnessed, nor to indulge in any activities that disrupt public life and the work of this government.

So spoke the President in a noon broadcast.

In a few days we were seeing Pitso off at the airport. He was bound for Botswana. The Botswana government gave him travel papers, on condition that he proceed as planned — across the border into South Africa. Which meant giving himself up to the Boers.

'Look after yourself now son of Africa,' Chieza said to him when I went to fetch our friend from the prison. 'You must do what you must. Make sure you have enough medicine for the bowels.'

'The gods of Chieza keep you too, son of Africa,' Pitso said.

He was silent all the way to the airport. I tried teasing him out of his mood. All he did was nod and smile weakly now and again. At the gates, he suddenly flung his thick arms around me. They trembled. 'Kwacha, Moyo! Keep the faith!'

When the plane took to the blue space above, tears gathered in my eyes. At the same time Studs Letanka's words returned to me: funerals without corpses . . . What can you tell me now Ambuye, and Letanka? Let me hear your voices — what have you to tell me? I'm listening . . .

'These two or three days since Pitso left I have been trying to push out of my mind a suggestion that I visit Chimba in jail. I decided to come over anyhow and if my heart told me to visit him first before I came to see you I would obey. My heart told me nothing, so I came straight here.'

Chieza nods a few times.

'Funny thing, no? I'm here and he's there — maybe in some VIP cell. And we're as far apart as Cape Town from Cairo. Strangers in the full glare of daytime. One hope came to me, you know, when Botswana offered Pitso a chance to live in their land — when he said no thanks, they still gave him papers — you know, Moyo?'

'A hope for what?'

'Maybe this halfwitted corkscrew of a warder is right shouting *kwacha!* every morning like a toy rooster. Maybe a bright new day never ceases to dawn — somewhere on this cursed globe — you see it or feel it or you don't. Er — your sister should be arriving any day now for the school of nursing, right?'

'Ya. But how can you say that — this about bright days — when you're kept in this cage?'

Chieza gives me a steady gaze. Then he shrugs his shoulders. 'About Chirundu,' he says instead, 'Are you afraid to go and see him?'

'I don't know what I feel. Yes — er — I think I *am* afraid somewhat. It's the kind of fear — I think — you know when you've got a killer of an animal in a cage — you know it can't break out — but you go and touch the wall of the cage — and something — something seems to tug at your nerves — you tremble ever so little — the slightest movement in the cage makes you jump or jerk or anything —'

'That's nothing, son of Mutiso — what bothers me is that they never let go once they have tasted power — they will lose now but they will always try to come back — maybe they think they're made for great things — handicaps like this one make them mad — they come back fighting, maybe meaner than ever before.'

It is my turn to shrug my shoulders.